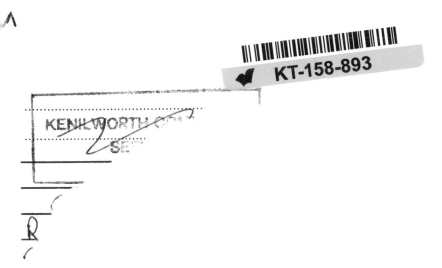

# The Land Grabbers

Old Harry Payne was a rogue who exploited everything and everybody. When he was killed in a shoot-out the world seemed well rid of him, but those responsible soon found themselves targets.

Then Harry's sons started a range war and hired a professional gun to keep the local ranchers off their land. Now the town of Coville was involved and a new marshal took up his guns. Yet the more he learned the more complicated the problem seemed.

There was destined to be a final shoot-out and the marshal had to sort it out his way – or die in the attempt.

# The Land Grabbers

Tom Benson

A Black Horse Western

ROBERT HALE · LONDON

© Tom Benson 2006
First published in Great Britain 2006

ISBN-10: 0-7090-7899-4
ISBN-13: 978-0-7090-7899-9

Robert Hale Limited
Clerkenwell House
Clerkenwell Green
London EC1R 0HT

Typeset by Derek Doyle & Associates, Shaw Heath.
Printed and bound in Great Britain by
Antony Rowe Limited, Wiltshire.

# ONE

The night was fine and dry in the Kansas town of Abilene. Lights shone from the windows to brighten up the rutted streets. It was the quiet season, when the main cattle runs were over and things were getting back to a peaceful level for the folks who lived on the right side of the rail-road tracks.

The Merchants' Hotel stood proud in its dominant position, with the lighted oil-lamp atop a square whitewashed pillar by the steps leading to the front door. The chairs on the stoop were empty. Patrons were either in bed or at one of the saloons where gambling and every other sort of entertainment would keep nearby Cedar Street busy until the early hours.

The two young men who crossed to the hotel were armed with shotguns. They also carried pistols at their waists and appeared to be looking for trouble. The few people on the street gazed at them with a certain wariness and then went about their business. The carrying of guns was forbidden by a town ordinance, but the Smith brothers always thought themselves above the law. And nobody was willing to argue.

They mounted the three wooden steps, threw open the door, and entered the quiet room where the reception desk stood empty under the lamplight. One of the brothers looked at the small brass bell on the desk-top. His companion nodded and he banged it with the palm of his hand. It sounded loud in the empty foyer.

A door opened near the rear stairs and an elderly man in shirt-sleeves came out with a welcoming smile on his pale face. It collapsed when he saw who was at the desk. A nervous hand went to his scraggy grey moustache as he placed the solid woodwork between himself and the two brothers.

'What can I be doin' for you, Mr Smith?' he asked in an uncertain voice.

The younger of the brothers spoke up. He was tall and thin, with dark features that suggested a hint of Mexican blood.

'You got a fella stayin' here by the name of Payne,' he said. 'Where is he?'

The little clerk swallowed noisily.

'He's out.'

'Where?'

It was the other brother who spoke. A slightly

stouter version of the first speaker, he was almost as dark and had one eye covered with a black patch.

'I think he's gone along to Cedar Street,' the clerk said in an effort to get them out of the hotel. 'Went off straight after his supper, he did.'

The older brother leaned across the desk and grabbed the little man by his collar.

'If you're tellin' lies, fella,' he said quietly, 'we'll be back. And this place will never look the same again. Neither will you.'

The two men turned on their heels and left the building. The little clerk leaned against the wall. His face was streaming with sweat and he trembled as he tried to wipe it away with a large bandanna. A well-dressed woman came down the stairs to look at him with narrowed eyes. She tapped an imperious finger on the desk to attract his attention.

'What's come over you, Pete?' she demanded in a loud voice. 'You look as if you've seen a ghost.'

'It's them Smith fellas, ma'am,' the clerk replied as he put away the bandanna. 'They came in with guns, lookin' for Mr Payne. I said he was over on Cedar Street.'

The owner pursed her lips thoughtfully.

'And is he?' she asked.

'I don't know, ma'am, but I was aimin' to get rid of them. They're dangerous fellas.'

'So is old Harry Payne if he's sober.'

She tapped her fingers on the desk uncertainly for a moment and then made up her mind.

'Let's play it safe, Pete,' she said. 'Go round to the marshal's office and tell him that the Smith brothers are on the prod. Then get back here and saddle Harry Payne's horse. Put some food and drink on it and have it ready round the back for him to make a clean break. I don't want folk saying we let an old friend down.'

The clerk headed for the door but the owner had a change of mind and called him back.

'On second thoughts,' she said, 'saddle the horse first just in case he turns up before the law gets here. Marshals ain't all that fast in cases like this. The Smith brothers ain't small boys throwing bricks at stray dogs.'

The man nodded and hurried off.

Harry Payne had already left Cedar Street. He swayed slightly as he walked back to his hotel but his eyes were alert despite their constant watering. His limp was more pronounced than usual and he breathed out a lush aroma of cheap whiskey. He was in his mid-sixties; a tough and lean old veteran of pioneering days and of the late war. He was a Southerner; a rancher, and a dissolute old rogue who did not intend to age gracefully. He had two sons to take over when he wanted time off. And he had the consolation of

8

knowing that a psalm-singing, disapproving wife was safely buried in the family plot at the H bar P spread.

He was a quietly dressed man, in a dark coat and starched white collar and shirt. There was a short-barrelled Colt hidden away and a steady enough hand to use it. He knew the law about firearms in Abilene, but Harry's respect for law was somewhat less than profound. His thin, well-shaven face was dominated by a sharp, beaked nose that was more often than not displaying a small dewdrop which vanished when he sniffed. The mouth was large and lascivious, and his grin had the infectious mischief of a naughty boy.

Harry was looking forward to his bed. The lamp on top of the tall pillar outside the hotel was like a beacon for a homecoming pilgrim. He headed for it along the wide, dusty street and had almost reached the steps when a familiar figure hove into sight.

It was the third Smith brother. He was fatter and older than the other two and walked with a roll that Harry remembered from past encounters. The man was tall and his dark face was only relieved by the pale-grey eyes that flickered across the street as he searched for his prey.

Harry was not afraid of the man, but he knew that if one of the brothers was about the others would not be far away. He glanced nervously round at the late-night revellers making their ways home. The street was dark, with only fitful streaks of light from the windows of the buildings and the steady glow from the pillar outside the hotel.

To his right was an alley between his destination and Herman Myer's clothing store. Harry walked quietly towards it, trying not to attract attention to himself. Once there he could reach the corrals where his horse was kept, or make it to the rear door of the hotel where he could get at his belongings and flee town before the brothers bunched up on him.

There was a sudden angry shout, and Harry knew that it was the oldest Smith brother who had seen him. He ran for the alley, pushing a couple of unsteady revellers out of his path. He was swallowed up in the complete darkness and ran as fast as his damaged leg would take him to reach the maze of corrals and outhouses behind the street.

Harry was sweating now and gasping for breath. The old wound was nagging at his leg as it always did when he was on foot and walking too much. He took out the Colt and turned left at the end of the little alley so that he was against the hotel wall. It was pitch-dark there with a moon totally hidden by heavy cloud.

The smell of the nearby horses was strong as he stumbled along the wooden walkboards, feeling for the rear door and hoping that it would

10

be open. A shot split the air and its flash lit up the spot where the Smith brother had emerged from the alley and had heard or seen something of Harry feeling his way along the wooden wall.

Harry fired back. He cocked the pistol to shoot again, but hesitated. He had no spare bullets and there were only five shots to begin with. Like all experienced gun-handlers, he never kept a cartridge under the hammer.

There was noise around him now. The shooting had spooked the horses and they were careering around their corrals. Lights were coming on in rear windows, and Harry stood silhouetted against the background. He cursed vividly and tried to edge further along to the door. He found the frame and felt around for the brass knob. His sweaty hand turned it, but nothing happened. He swore under his breath and moved to face the man who was now coming along the worn boardwalk with lumbering strides. They could see each other plainly and Harry raised the gun to defend himself.

What happened next took both of them by surprise. One of the corral gates swung open and the disturbed horses headed for freedom. An elderly man was with them, waving his coat and shouting. The animals filled the space behind the hotel, moving off wildly and brushing against the boardwalk so that their hoofs echoed as they struck the wooden planks. Harry

11

cowered against the wall as they passed him and he could see his big assailant doing the same.

One of the animals was harnessed and bore his saddle-bags on the crupper. Harry recognized his own gelding and realized that someone from the hotel had been trying to help him. He took advantage of the confusion and limped further along the rear of the building until he found the next alley that led back to the main street. He hurried down it and emerged amid the crowd that was gathering.

It was noisy as one of the deputy marshals pushed his way through and headed for the alley by Myer's clothing store. He vanished down it and Harry stood uncertainly among the bustling throng. He wondered whether he could get into the hotel and hide, or try and steal another horse and leave town.

The decision was made for him. Two figures appeared at the far end of the street as the other Smith brothers came back from their search. They spotted Harry and one of them let out a yell that was partly lost in the surrounding noise. Harry took to his heels and pushed his way through the crowd in the direction the deputy had taken.

A volley of shots rang out and everything was confusion. There was panic in the street as women screamed and men shouted aimlessly. The deputy returned to the mouth of the alley, his shotgun cocked and uncertainty written on his young face. The two Smith brothers fled the scene as a suddenly silent crowd gathered round a dying man.

'Who is he?' the deputy asked as he looked down at the twitching body.

There was a shaking of heads until the proprietor of the hotel pushed her way through the crowd and took a limp hand into her own warm grasp.

'It's a rancher from the south. His name's Harry Payne,' she said quietly.

# TWO

The funeral was well attended. The burial plot at the H bar P spread was on a slight hill that looked down on the comfortable home of the Payne family. All the locals had turned out, even travelling ten miles or more to be there. Some said with a certain truth that they only attended to make sure that the old rogue was dead. But Harry had plenty of real friends and there was a certain tension in the air at his killing.

The casket had arrived after a ten-day journey of over a hundred miles to reach the final resting-place. It was lined with lead and accompanied by a letter from the marshal of Abilene, telling of the events that caused the old man's death. Ma Ridgely, the owner of the hotel, had arranged things for the family. She had known the Paynes for years and made sure that the local mortician did a good job for them. She also sent a letter, but telling a slightly different story from that given by the marshal.

It was a warm day but with a slight breeze that rustled the dark skirts of the women. The preacher held forth in his usual fashion while folk looked round at each other rather than pay attention to his well-worn rhetoric. Harry's two sons stood side by side. Joe was the elder; a thirtyish copy of his father with the same large, lascivious mouth and sharp eyes that missed very little. Fred was a slighter figure, narrow-shouldered and called a simpleton by his late father. He had married young and his wife now stood at his side.

Betty ran his life for him and, being the only woman on the spread, she ran the domestic side of things without interference. She was a fine-looking lass with two growing children and another on the way. She could shoot as well as any man and cuss when necessary. Fred had enough sense never to argue with her, and even Joe was wary after one encounter that left him with a bruised lip and swollen eye.

The preacher droned on as an elderly man watched from the base of the slope. His clothes were dusty and his horse looked as if it had made a long journey. The man had not shaved for days and he chewed tobacco thoughtfully as he watched what was happening at the burial plot. When the mourners started their tuneless singing about all meeting beyond the river, he snorted his disgust and led the horse away towards the ranch house.

It was a large place flanked by other buildings to form three sides of a square. There were rocking-chairs on the stoop and the windows shone brightly in front of white curtains. The old man tethered his horse at the rail and entered the building. The main room was clean and smelled fresh. A long table was laid out with the funeral feasts and he sampled some of the food. Then he poured himself a large glass of whiskey from a supply on the sideboard. After wiping his lips and taking a careful look round, he went out again and led the horse away.

The mourners had departed. All of them well fed and some of them sober. Fred and Joe sat by the stove, their feet stuck out towards the warm metal and tin mugs of whiskey in their grasps. Betty had put the children to bed and sat at the table to work with needle and thread at the large quilt that seemed to occupy all her leisure time. They were all taken by surprise when the door opened and a figure stood there, clutching saddle-bags and a Winchester rifle. Betty stifled a little cry and Fred half-rose from his chair, spilling the whiskey over his foot.

'You're late, Pa,' Joe said with a grin. 'You missed your own funeral.'

Old Harry entered the room, dumped the

bags on the floor and crossed to the stove to pick up the pot of coffee.

'I ain't missed nothing,' he said with a sigh of content. 'You sure as hell gave me one good send-off, and I'm right grateful. Did Ma Ridgley tell you what happened in Abilene?'

'Sent a note, Pa,' Joe explained. 'Said there was a shoot-out with the Smiths and some old fella got killed in all the confusion. She told folks it was you, had the body moved to the hotel and togged up in your other coat. The Smiths went away satisfied and daren't go back to Abilene 'cos there's a warrant out for them.'

'Ma Ridgley's a good friend,' Harry chuckled. 'Did she send my horse back?'

'It arrived with your body, And your saddle-bags. We got one hell of a bill from the mortician and the transport folks. You're all done up in the finest lead-lined casket in the territory.'

Harry nodded slowly and sipped the hot coffee.

'I had to steal a horse to get outa Abilene,' he said. 'How many folks know that I'm still alive?'

'Nobody, Pa.' Joe grinned. 'I reckoned as how you might want to lie low until the Smiths forget about you.'

'We should go gunnin' for them, Pa,' Fred said angrily. 'They sure need a good hammerin' for killin' you.'

Harry looked pityingly at his younger son.

'Maybe they do, boy,' he murmured, 'but they got three big spreads and have about thirty guns between them. We can probably muster seven or eight if old Steve is sober. If the Smiths hear that I'm still in the land of the living, they'll be down on this place faster than you can spit. No, we gotta keep this quiet. I aim to square up with the Smiths in my own way, and in my own time. I'm dead, and that's the way I'm stayin' until them three fellas join me in hell.'

Joe nodded shrewdly.

'How you goin' to go about it, Pa?' he asked quietly.

Harry looked round the comfortable room before replying.

'Well, now,' he said slowly, 'if I'm dead, then you two fellas have taken on the H bar P spread. So I'm gonna go stay with Uncle Jesse up near Watona township. I'll have another name and I'm lettin' this beard grow a little more. You'll send me a monthly pension, just like I was some retired city fella who quit his high-falutin job. You'll pay it into our local bank to the account of Bill Dean. Every month on the dot.'

'Won't the bank ask questions, Pa?' Joe asked.

'No. I already got an account under that name in Watona.'

Fred was frowning as he thought over the situation. 'Do you mean you already got two names

18

and two places to live, Pa?' he asked in puzzlement.

'You're quick off the mark, lad.' Harry
grinned. 'I ain't no simpleton and I've made a
few enemies. I always reckoned it might be good
plannin' to vanish one day. Another hideout,
another bank, and another name.'

His daughter-in-law looked at the old devil
with grim admiration.

'You're one crooked dealer, Harry Payne,' she
said.

'I bin workin' at it for years, lass. Now, you
fellas will run this spread at a profit and keep me
supplied with cash money. I'll be makin' trips up
north now and then to pick off the Smith brothers one at a time. If we need to get in touch with
each other, add ten dollars to the monthly
payment. That'll be my signal to come here. If I
want to get in touch with you, I'll just turn up
like I did tonight. Understood?'

They all nodded and Joe brought out the jug
of corn mash for a taste of something stronger
than coffee. He passed it round before asking
any more questions. When the jug was recorked,
Joe leaned across the table.

'Now, Pa,' he asked in a solemn tone, 'in the
midst of all this shootin' at folks, did you manage
to do what you intended to do in Abilene?'

Harry grinned. 'I sure did, son. In more ways
than one. The word is out that the price of beef

will be up next season. They've got cattle disease in the north and there's been real dry weather there. The railroad is gonna need animals from down here, and there are big army contracts to be placed as well. Next season could be the best for years.'

Joe nodded contentedly. Then his eyes narrowed.

'The other local spreads will be usin' our water again, Pa,' he said grimly. 'And our pasture. It ain't right, the way they drive their herds over H bar P land without as much as a howdydo.'

Harry shrugged. 'Always been that way,' he said. 'If they don't use our valley and the creek there, it'd be another three or four days on the trail to the railhead. Just part of bein' neighbourly.'

'I figure as how we could delay them or charge a few cents a head for goin' through the valley and usin' our water supply,' Joe said. He looked hard at his father and the two men seemed to pass some unspoken message.

'You're runnin' things now, son,' Harry answered. 'Your old man's dead and buried.'

Fred had been sitting quietly with the tin cup of corn mash in his hands. He was a young man who was slow to put his thoughts into any sort of order.

'You could make peace with the Smiths, Pa,'

he said slowly. 'Then we could get back to normal.'

The old man looked at him pityingly.

'Jeannie Smith is a rich woman, lad,' he explained carefully. 'When old man Smith died he divided his spread between her brothers and Jeannie. Her husband already had land of his own, so now she's a widow-woman, she has a mighty fine ranch under her control. Now her brothers ain't got no wives. No decent woman will have them. The chances are that she'll get their land as well. And they're as scared as hell that some handsome buck will come along and carry her off. And I'm the handsome buck they have in mind.'

Joe grinned at the familiar story.

'And I reckon you aim to do just that, Pa,' he said.

'I ain't sayin' as how I'm averse to marryin' up with a well-preserved widow-woman. And her lands would sure as hell make us Paynes the biggest ranchers in these parts. Talkin' peace with her brothers ain't part of the story. They don't aim to see her marry nobody. They want that land and they figure as how their pa should never have left her a share in the first case.'

Fred nodded slowly and thought it over. He looked at his wife for inspiration.

'Jeannie Jones, or Smith as she was born, is in her fifties, Pa,' she said quietly. 'She's apt to

21

outlive you. What happens to Joe and Fred then?'

'They'd be runnin' the spreads and I figure as how they're big enough to look out for themselves,' Harry said as he glanced slyly at Joe. 'Besides, I aim to live a few more years yet and an agein' widow-woman ain't no match for you three. After all, she's got no kin.'

'Other than her three brothers,' Betty said bluntly.

Harry nodded grimly. 'And I'm goin' huntin' in the next week or so. Baggin' myself a few trophies. Just think of it, lads. All them spreads belongin' to us. We'd be the richest folk in the entire territory.'

He looked round the table at the attentive faces of his family. Harry knew that he and Joe saw things the same way and that Fred would simply follow the lead of the others. Betty was a smart girl and had a fine head on her young shoulders. He was leaving the ranch in safe hands.

'Now, I'll need some cash money,' he said briskly, 'and enough food to get me to Uncle Jesse's place. It's three days or more from here and I don't aim to starve on the way. I'll also need a jug of whiskey to make the old fella feel real hospitable.'

'What sort of spread does Uncle Jesse have, Pa?' Fred asked.

'Nothin' worth speakin' of. He just keeps hogs to sell for meat and lives quiet-like since Mary passed on. Folk don't bother him and I'll be able to stay there without anyone knowin' who the hell I really am. Folk round there know me as Bill Dean. I'll rest up here for a few hours and light out early in the mornin' before the hands are awake. I'll have to keep the horse I got now in case they notice that one of our animals is missing. It ain't that I don't trust our folks, but they do go into town and take a drink when we pay them each month. So, let's get to bed.'

Betty had been standing by the table with a mug in her hand. She was like a statue, immobile and her face looked alert as though to some danger.

'What's upsettin' you, girl?' Harry asked quietly.

'There's someone outside, Pa,' she answered.

Harry cursed and jumped up from his chair. His hand went automatically to the gun at his side. Then he sat down again.

'Go see who it is, lads,' he ordered tersely. 'It may be one of the hands usin' the privy and wonderin' why the light's still on in here. He probably ain't seen me, but check on it.'

His two sons collected shotguns and headed for the door. Betty put down the mug and came round the table to where her father-in-law sat.

'He looked in at the window, Pa,' she said. 'I

could see him through the curtains, and it ain't one of our people.'

Harry rose and went to peer into the darkness that was relieved only by the light from the building and the brilliance of the stars that shone in a cloudless sky.

There was a yell as Joe shouted at someone to stop. It was answered by a shot that came from near the old disused well. Fred levelled his shotgun and loosed both barrels. Another shot rang out and the bullet could almost be felt as it hit the wooden building where Harry and Betty watched. Joe ran across the yard and fired his own shotgun. He did not aim, but let both barrels fly as he ducked for cover behind a water-trough.

His shot was effective and a figure stumbled from the shelter of the well, wobbling uncertainly for a few paces before collapsing. The two Payne brothers ran across and turned the body over to see who the intruder was. Lights were going on in the bunkhouse and Harry could hear his elder son telling the wakened hands that they had caught a prowler who was probably trying to steal horses.

The old man moved back from the window and sat in a corner of the room where he was less likely to be seen if the door opened. He was relying on Joe to handle their employees and quieten things down again.

Several minutes passed while Betty and Harry sat anxiously without speaking. The door eventually opened and the two brothers entered with the empty shotguns under their arms and a collection of items they had taken from the dead man.

'Well?' Harry's voice was edgy.

'Must have just been a prowler, Pa,' Joe said cheerfully. 'Seven dollars, one pretty old .44 with a matchin' Winchester. Some chewin' tobacco and a harmonica. I reckon him as bein' about fifty and his horse had a saddle-bag with plenty of food in it. There's a bedroll and a slicker. That's about it.'

Harry looked at the articles they had dumped on the table. His lips were pursed thoughtfully. It was too much of a coincidence that a prowler was around the ranch house on the very night he came home.

'Any brand on his horse?' he asked.

'Yeah. One I never came across before. An M over a J.'

Harry let out a sigh that was almost one of relief. His face broke into its usual cheeky grin.

'Well, if that don't beat all,' he wheezed happily. 'The brand of the late Mel Jones. Jeannie has sent one of her hands to make sure I'm dead.'

# THREE

The marshal of Coville spent most of his time sitting on the stoop in front of the jailhouse. His feet were on the hitching-rail as he rocked gently back and forth in the warmth of the dry, long days. He had a peaceful town where the mayor owned one of the saloons, bought most of the votes with free drinks, and where folk prospered from the ranches all around.

Matt Perry was a middle-aged man, running to fat and blaming his wife for that. She fed him too well, he complained, but he never refused the succulent meals she put on the table. Today was much like any other. The main street was busy and the stores had windows that sparkled in the sunlight and displayed goods that came from the big cities.

The bank was prosperous. The hardware and food stores did a thriving business, while the stage came twice a week as it passed through from other towns. Coville had a telegraph office and two fine hotels. It was a town that was going places, and some folk predicted that the railroad would one day run alongside it on the way west to the developing territories.

Marshal Perry did not pay much attention to the wagon that was unloading outside Ted West's hardware store. He was barely conscious of the four heavy horses that champed at their feed-bags while heavy rolls of something wrapped in canvas sacking were carried in by several men.

It was the mayor who broke his reverie. Nathan Laird had been standing in front of the Southern Star saloon for some time. He had seen the wagon arrive at the store opposite and was curious about the cargo it carried. He was tempted to cross the street to find out, but hesitated in case folk might think that he was being too nosy.

The mayor was a big man, well dressed in a black frock-coat and pale suede waistcoat. His watch chain was of heavy gold and his round, pleasant face was set off by a neat moustache that was as dyed as his hair. He had a fine paunch to add to the general look of well-being. Beneath the veneer was a different personality. He was a hard political figure with no scruples about achieving power and the wealth that went with it.

He watched as the last of the heavy bundles

was carried into the store. The driver came out, took the feed-bags off the horses, and climbed up to drive away. The mayor knew where he was from. He had made a journey of several days from another town where freight wagons ran a regular service from the railhead. It was all part of the expanding prosperity of the region and he was proud to be connected with it. It was making him rich.

Nathan Laird glanced down the street to where the marshal lay sprawled in his rocker. He hesitated for a moment as he thought about letting the lawman go across to the hardware store. Then he plucked up courage and decided to make his own enquiries. He walked majestically across the rutted street and entered the dim, cool building that smelt of lamp-oil and soap. The canvas bundles were already being moved to the rear storeroom by Ted West's son. He rolled them across the floor with a certain careful touch that suggested they might be dangerous.

'I just looked in to see if my new copper lamp had arrived,' the mayor lied cheerfully. 'I saw the freight wagon leaving.'

Ted West shook his head.

'Another week or two, Mayor,' he said. 'It's gotta come all the way from Chicago, and that's one hell of a journey. This is all they delivered today.'

28

He waved a hand at the large bundles and the mayor looked at them as though noting their presence for the first time.

'What on earth are those things?' he asked in idle curiousity.

'Barbed wire.'

The words were a shock and the mayoral mouth fell open in hurt surprise. He had heard of the stuff but never actually seen a coil of it before. He bent over to touch one of the bundles and could feel the well-wrapped barbs under the heavy sacking. There was a label tied with string that told the world that it was Glidden's patent steel barbed wire. Galvanized.

'What in the name of thunder do we want with that stuff?' he asked in a broken voice. 'Are you expecting homesteaders or something?'

The squat, dark-browed hardware dealer grinned as he shook his head.

'They're all for the H bar P spread,' he said happily. 'A fine big order from the Payne brothers. They're sure as hell spendin' money now that their pa's dead.'

The mayor looked at the bundles.

'They must be,' he muttered. 'But what does a ranch want with barbed wire? There are no sheep- or hog-breeders near their spread. And no homesteaders that I hear tell of. They need a free range, so it doesn't make sense.'

He moved nearer to the storekeeper, towering

over him as he asked the vital question.

'What are they up to, Ted?'

The man shrugged with complete indifference.

'I don't know, Mayor,' he admitted, 'but they ordered all this stuff and they're gonna pay cash on the barrel. It ain't for the likes of me to go askin' them questions.'

The mayor pushed one of the bundles with a delicately shod foot.

'I don't like this, Ted,' he muttered uneasily. 'Barbed wire could mean trouble somewhere or other. These Payne lads are not the brightest candles in the cabin. What in hell's name can they be up to?'

The storekeeper shrugged again.

'They'll be collectin' the stuff in the next day or two,' he said cheerfully. 'You can ask them yourself then.'

'Well, if Joe comes into town I will certainly do so. But Fred won't be much help. He's got less sense than a dead mule, and he's a little too happy with a gun. We could talk it over if their pa was here. Harry Payne was always a reasonable sort of fellow to deal with.'

'He was an old rogue,' the dealer snorted.

'I grant you that,' the mayor conceded handsomely, 'but he didn't go around antagonizing his neighbours. Except over women, of course. They're going to use this wire for fencing of some sort and the other ranchers are not going to take kindly to that.'

Nathan Laird walked slowly back across the street and made for the marshal's office. The lawman was now chewing tobacco and spitting at any insect within firing-range.

'Do you know anything about this barbed wire business?' the mayor asked bluntly.

The man shook his head in puzzlement and had to be told about the delivery that had just taken place under his nose.

'Ask around town,' he was ordered. 'Be discreet about it, but find out what you can.'

The marshal did not know the meaning of some of the mayor's fancy words, but he nodded reluctant obedience and watched Nathan Laird's stately progress back to the Southern Star saloon. He pondered the problem and came to the conclusion that by visiting the Southern Star and the other saloon he would be able to dig up some information. And then there was the telegraph clerk. He was sworn to secrecy but always obliged the marshal with any titbit he came across in the course of his duties. Matt Perry sighed heavily at the responsibilities of high office.

Things began to move a couple of days later. A wagon rolled into town, driven by Fred Payne and with his brother sitting up on the box at his side. They reined in the two mules outside the hardware store and both men got down and entered the building. The marshal was in his usual seat outside the jailhouse. He had dutifully spent time drinking and playing cards but knew nothing more than he had known on the first day. He watched the two ranchers uneasily. They were rich men, both handy with guns, and Fred was quick-tempered if somebody pushed too hard.

He was just about to move reluctantly from his chair when he saw the mayor coming out of the saloon and crossing purposefully to Ted West's store. Marshal Perry decided to leave it to the First Citizen. He would just keep a watching brief.

Mayor Laird was just in time to see the first of the sacking-covered rolls being brought from the back storeroom. Joe was at the counter, handing money over to Ted West while Fred helped the lad to load the wagon.

'Good morning, Joe,' the mayor boomed in his best political voice. 'Nice to see you in town. And you, Fred. How's the family?'

Joe finished counting the notes before acknowledging the newcomer.

'Betty and the kids are well,' he said politely. 'And how are you, Mr Mayor?'

'Coping with life, Joe. Just coping.' The mayor's eyes were straying to the two men moving the barbed wire.

'I'm a mite surprised to see you needing all that stuff, Joe,' he said in a more serious voice. 'There hasn't been any call for it round here in the past.'

Joe smiled slightly as he tucked a receipt into his pocket. 'And you want to know what we're gonna be fencin' in?' he suggested.

'Well – the question does spring to mind, and the range has always been free – and neighbourly.'

'Still is, but Fred and me have to move with the times. Pa was set in his ways, but we aim to make ranchin' pay real well. And one of the ways of doin' that is to give ourselves a head start on other folks when the drive north begins.'

The mayor blinked and opened his mouth to say more. Then the meaning of the words sank home.

'You're going to close Twin Buttes,' he said unbelievingly.

Joe nodded. 'That's right. Save the water and grazin' for our own cattle and give us a few days' start to the railhead. That's business, Mr Mayor.'

Ted West and Nathan Laird looked at each other. The hardware store-owner glanced at the money in his hand with a sudden expression of guilt before recovering his composure enough to put it firmly in the cash drawer.

'Your pa would never have done a thing like

that, Joe,' the mayor said sadly. 'He always let folk use the valley.'

'Pa's dead,' the young man replied bluntly, 'and we gotta make the ranch pay. Times is hard, Mayor, and every season we have to stand by and watch other folks' cattle cross our land, eat up our pasture, and use our water supply. And not so much as a howdydo from any of them. If they can't go through Twin Buttes, it'll make a difference of four or five days to their drive north. That would give us a start to the railhead and the best prices. That's just plain sense, Mayor. That's business.'

'It's dirty business, Joe,' the First Citizen replied angrily. 'Your family have been here since early days, but this could leave you without a friend to your name. It could even start a range war. Do you realize that?'

Joe nodded. 'That's up to them,' he said. 'It's my land, my water, and I ain't seein' other folk killin' off the pasture. I figure on their cattle gettin' to market carryin' less weight than mine, and gettin' there later.'

Ted West decided to put in a few words.

'Suppose they start a week or so earlier, Joe'?' he suggested. 'They could take the longer route.'

'They'd still be underweight,' Joe assured him. 'But don't misunderstand me, Mayor. We ain't stoppin' folk usin' the Twin Buttes valley.

We're just stoppin' herds of cattle goin' through on the way to the railhead.'

Nathan Laird grimaced.

'That's almighty kind of you, Joe,' he said quietly, 'but there are more than ten spreads that use that route. With your pa gone, I figure as how you only have about nine guns all told to stop them. I know Betty can shoot, but even ten guns against a whole county and beyond won't amount to very much. Is it really worth all that trouble?'

Joe grinned.

'I got one thing they ain't got, Mayor,' he said cheerfully. 'I've got Black Jack Neville.'

# FOUR

Winston Crossing was hardly a town. It only existed because of the shallow river that narrowed at its curve and enabled a ferry to convey travellers across the fast-flowing water. There was a general store, a few houses of adobe or wood, and a small brick building that served as chapel and school. The saloon was the busiest place. It gloried in the name of the Golden Nugget and catered for local ranchers who came in each weekend to sample the warm beer and cheap whiskey.

A few obliging girls occupied a couple of rooms above and one of them was now at the bar, talking to a tall, thin man whose dark features gave a hint of Mexican blood. He was clutching a whiskey-glass and leaned close to the girl as they whispered to each other. It being a Saturday night, the saloon was busy and nobody paid any heed to the unwashed old tramp who stood at the far end with a glass of cloudy beer in his gnarled hand. He leaned on the counter, taking no notice of what went on around him, but his eyes were deceptive as they gazed apparently into space to some point behind the bar.

It was a mirror he stared at. It was angled in such a way that he could see the young man who was talking to the girl. If anyone had paid attention they would have noticed that the old man hardly drank and that his eyes seldom left the mirror.

The tall young fellow and the girl suddenly finished their drinks and headed for the stairs. The bartender winked at the other drinkers while the old man slowly sipped his beer. Two card-players started quarrelling across the saloon but it ended when the owner came out of a back room and made some quiet remark to them. He was a large man with a scarred face and a handy gun at his belt. They were not going to argue.

It was not long before the young man came down the stairs again and headed for the door. He untethered his horse, tightened the girth, and rode down the dark street. The old man at the bar finished his drink in a hurry and followed. He did not bother to keep his quarry in sight as they left town. He seemed to know where the man was heading.

The moon peeked out behind the high cloud for a time and made the going easier. They were on a well-worn trail and the only movement was from the creatures of the night who scurried across the ground in search of food.

It was the best part of two hours before the young man reined in his horse near a clump of bushes and began to prepare camp. He lit a fire, took the blanket from the crupper of his mount, and started to make himself comfortable for the night. The fire threw dancing shadows as moths came to flit among the tall flames. The man lay back with head resting on the saddle and a small bottle in his right hand. He did not bother to make a meal but was quite happy with what was left of the whiskey in the bottle.

The old man watched from a distance. His prey was silhouetted by the light of the fire as he slipped the Colt .44 from its holster and quietly pulled back the hammer. He saw the young man throw away the empty bottle and roll over on his side to sleep. With a wry grin on his whiskered face he raised the gun and took careful aim. It was centred perfectly on the back of the man who lay before the fire.

Then the old man hesitated and after some moments lowered the weapon. He muttered an audible curse as he stood up and stepped out into the firelight. The young man scrambled to his feet and found himself facing a drawn gun.

'Who the hell are you, fella?' he demanded in a slightly quavering voice.

38

'I'm somebody who aims to kill you,' his opponent said quietly. 'You and them other two rattlers called Smith.'

The young man peered at his enemy in the flickering light. His hand was within a few inches of the gun at his side but he seemed to hesitate about risking a draw.

'Why?' he asked. 'We ain't done you no harm that I knows of. And I ain't worth robbin' after a night in town. I don't carry more than a few dollars. So in hell's name, why?'

'Because you killed me.'

'We. . . ?'

The young Smith brother looked stunned. He shook his head in bewilderment as well as to shake it clear of the whiskey.

'Who the hell are you, fella?' he asked. 'I just don't know you.'

'I'm the man you killed in Abilene.'

There was a moment of silence before young Alex Smith got his thoughts back together.

'That ain't possible. That was old Harry Payne. He was killed right there on the street and everybody saw it. They've buried him back on his spread.'

'Some other fella got shot,' Harry told him cheerfully, 'and I had enough friends in Abilene to help me get outa town while they told folk it were me as got killed by three brave fellas called Smith. But there ain't three of you now. Just you

39

and me, and I got the draw on you.'

'You're gonna kill all three of us? Fella, you'll never live long enough to do it. Abie and Ned will sure as hell get you as soon as they hear about me.'

Harry grinned. 'You won't be tellin' them, Alex,' he said quietly. 'Shootin' me was a bad idea. I got a vengeful nature, just like you fellas.'

Alex Smith was sweating.

'We was scared, Harry. Scared you'd be marryin' Jeannie and takin' her share of Pa's spread. We wanted to keep it in the family. And then there was the ranch she got from her husband. Abie didn't want to lose that either. It was all his idea. Me and Ned just went along with it. Look, Harry, let's just call it a mistake, and forget the whole thing. We'll laugh at this in a few years' time.'

'If you want to draw that piece, go right ahead, 'cos I'm pullin' the trigger as soon as your hand moves.'

'That ain't a fair draw, Harry.'

'Three against one ain't a fair draw either.'

Harry raised the barrel of the Colt a little and his finger pressed the trigger. The gun kicked and the flash lit the scene for a moment. Alex Smith staggered backward, then recovered. The shot had taken him in the left arm as he raised it to protect his body. His right hand drew the gun at his side and the noise of the hammer was loud as he aimed at Harry and fired.

But Harry had moved a little to the left and fired again. His bullet took Alex Smith full in the chest and the man reeled back in a slight spin before collapsing on his face. The old man crossed over to the body and stirred it with his foot.

'One down, two to go,' he muttered.

# FIVE

The mayor of Coville called the meeting to order. It was not a difficult thing to do so early in the day. The councilmen were still sober and had only just seated themselves in his large office. They had been supplied with whiskey and cigars to ensure obedience, and Nathan Laird was ready to discuss affairs in a way that would guarantee the acceptance of his views.

'Now, gentlemen,' he said in his best official voice, 'I have the accounts for the work carried out on the jailhouse, and I think we all agree that Phil Meadows did a good job. So all in favour of paying the bill?'

He looked around in a perfunctory manner and took it that they did all agree. He then moved on to several other items of business, which all passed scrutiny with equal ease and profit to various members of the council, including himself.

'Well, I think that just about covers everything,' the mayor summed up, 'so we'll meet again in a month's time to make a decision about the new books for the schoolhouse. All agreed?'

'What about this fella the Paynes are bringin' in? This Black Jack Neville?' somebody asked.

There was a murmur from the other councilmen and the mayor held up a podgy hand for silence.

'It may never happen,' he said gently. 'My own opinion is that the whole thing is a bluff to stop the other ranchers making a fuss about being delayed on their way to the railhead. I'm pretty certain that Joe and Fred will have second thoughts by the time the season starts.'

'They've spent a hell of a lot of money on that wire stuff,' one of the councilmen said sourly. 'That's one almighty big bluff in my book. What did the marshal report?'

'Well, he's been out to Twin Buttes three times now, as you have previously heard. No work has been done there, nor is there any sign of Black Jack being around the ranch. The hands were in town last weekend and I made a few discreet enquiries. I think it's all a bluff. I did warn Joe that blocking off that valley could start a range war. I have a feeling that my warning was enough to put an end to the affair.'

Doc Hawson dropped some cigar ash on the

floor as he cleared his throat.

'Who the hell is Black Jack Neville?' he asked in his creaky voice.

They all looked at him in surprise.

'You've never heard tell of him?' a storekeeper asked.

'Nope. He ain't one of my failures.'

'He's a hired gun,' the mayor explained. 'Keeps reasonably within the law and never shoots unless the other fellow is armed and able to draw. Seems that he prides himself on that. But he's one almighty killer, and once hired, he stays loyal. A dangerous man, Doc, and if the Paynes have taken him on, nobody round here is going to argue the point.'

'But you doubt that they've hired him?' the medical man suggested.

The mayor nodded.

'I doubt it. Nothing has happened out on their spread and the marshal is there now, taking another look around.'

'And why the fancy name?' Doc Hawson asked.

The other men gave nervous giggles.

'He's a tall, thin fella and dresses all in black like some dime storybook villain,' Ted West said. 'Not that I've read any of that hogswill,' he added hastily. 'But that's what they tell me.'

There was a long pause in the room and Nathan Laird decided to put an end to the meeting. Just as he was framing his announcement, the bank manager gave a loud cough. They all looked at this normally silent member of the council.

Will Fortnum was a solidly built man who dressed soberly and was respected but heartily disliked by nearly everybody. Too many people needed his services, and his bank screwed them for all it could get. They turned to face him now, their hostile looks not making any impression on the well-fed, smooth-faced moneylender.

'I think they have hired him,' he said calmly.

'How do you know?' the mayor asked anxiously.

'Well, I would not normally mention this, but ever since Harry Payne's death I have been sending a sum of money every month to another bank. I suspect that it represents the wages for this Black Jack fellow. He's going to turn up any day now.'

He looked round with a slight nervousness not usual with so confident a man.

'You understand,' he said with a certain diffidence, 'that under ordinary circumstances, I would not breach customer confidence. But this is different. If the Paynes cut off that valley, our town could suffer.'

'So could your bank,' somebody muttered unkindly.

Ted West leaned forward and drew their attention.

'We could outbid the Paynes,' he suggested.

'He's already taken their money so I doubt it would work,' Nathan Laird murmured. 'But we can try it when we meet up with the man.'

'Better let the marshal make the suggestion,' the banker said shrewdly. 'A violent man might take it badly, and none of us is a gunslinger.'

They all nodded agreement and the meeting broke up.

Mayor Laird watched them go off down the street before doing the next chore of his day. He checked his gold watch before going up to his living-quarters, having a word with his stout wife, and then picking up the small carpetbag that she had carefully packed for him. There was also a little tin box of food and she helped carry his burdens down to the back door where his buggy was waiting. She had already harnessed the horse and it was tossing its head up and down as it explored the feed-bag.

The mayor kissed his wife a perfunctory farewell, took off the feed-bag, and climbed up to the driving-seat. The vehicle protested at his enormous weight but the horse pulled willingly as they headed out of town.

He had the best part of a four-hour journey to the Double W ranch. It was a reasonably large spread south of town and old Wally Williams was a man who kept things neat and disciplined. His three sons were afraid of him, and so were the hands. Only his wife stood up to his temper, and she was tough enough to make him back off.

His ranch house was a clean-looking place set apart from the other buildings and on a gentle slope that gave a long view of distant hills and feeding cattle.

The mayor was welcomed with hot coffee as he sat down to wait for the three other local ranchers who had arranged to meet. They arrived one by one. Elijah Bowen was a bandy-legged man under middle height, but with the build of a fighter and a face that had been battered by many a brawl. Hugh Evans struck a contrasting note with dress that made him look like a preacher. He had the sour features to match and never touched tobacco or alcohol. The last man was from the Circle M. Hank Marwood had a reputation as a ruthless pioneer, and was among the first to settle the area before the war. He was in his sixties but had a full head of grey hair and a neat beard.

They all sat round the large table and, as if by common consent, waited for the mayor to conduct affairs.

'You've all heard about Black Jack Neville,' Nathan Laird said bluntly. 'I've told the folk back in town that the Paynes are bluffing and he won't be on his way. I could be wrong, and Will Fortnum tells me that they're already paying him a monthly wage. The question is now a simple one. What are you going to do about it?'

It was Elijah Bowen who spoke first. His twisted face was reddish as he spat out the words.

'We get all the hands together,' he snarled, 'and tear down their wire. Then shoot the hell outa the bastards.'

He looked round the table but there was not the response he expected.

'My men won't fight,' Wally Williams said sadly. 'When they heard in town that Black Jack was arriving, they got real nervous. Quittin' nervous.'

Hank Marwood ran a blotchy hand over his trim beard.

'I got much the same answer,' he said quietly, 'but there's other ways of skinin' a jackrabbit.'

He turned to the mayor.

'Are your folk keepin' a watch for the arrival of strangers?'

'I've got the marshal out at Twin Buttes right now, and if Neville hits town there are enough people there to recognize him. You want I should let you know?'

'As soon as he's seen,' Hank Marwood said. 'And just to be on the safe side I'll send my youngest boy out to the valley to keep a watch for strangers.'

'And what are you plannin' to do?'

It was the dry, high voice of Hugh Evans, who looked at the other ranchers with a certain disdain.

'I aim to save us all one hell of a lotta money,' Hank told him bluntly. 'And I aim to do it with as little loss of blood as possible.'

'Amen to that,' the austere man said, with pious eyes turned towards the ceiling.

The meeting broke up shortly afterwards and they sat down to a meal. While the others lounged around smoking their stogies, the self-righteous Mr Evans left the room to avoid the smoke and whiskey fumes. They watched him go, then turned their attention to Hank Marwood.

'What you got in mind?' the mayor asked quietly.

'There's no reason why Jack Neville should ever set foot on the Payne spread,' the bearded rancher said grimly. 'As soon as we know he's around, we can deal with him. One good shot and the Payne lads will have second thoughts about wirin' the range.'

'I shouldn't be hearing things like this,' Nathan Laird said primly.

Wally Williams grinned as he raised his glass to Hank.

'Maybe you shouldn't,' he chuckled, 'but it's what you came here to be told. After all, Nathan, that marshal of your'n is less damned use than a dead racoon.' He turned to Hank Marwood. 'Who's doin' the shooting?'

'I'll do it myself. That way I know it's done.

And I don't want that fool lawman within seein' distance while I'm about it.'

Nathan Laird nodded agreement.

'I'll call him off as soon as we know Black Jack is around,' he said. 'Though I still have doubts about him coming.'

They broke up shortly afterwards and the mayor decided to head back home instead of staying the night. It was late evening when he arrived, and after he had greeted his wife and corralled the horse, he went through to the saloon. There were still a few drinkers there and he looked around for Marshal Perry.

There was no sign of him and the bartender shook his head when asked if the lawman had been in. Nathan Laird frowned. He should have been back in town by now, and the saloon was the place he would head for by the instinct bred of years of experience.

The mayor walked along to the marshal's office. The door swung open but the place was in darkness and he had to strike a vesta to light the overhead lamp. There was no fire in the stove and Nathan Laird felt a sudden uneasiness as he looked around. He opened one of the drawers in the desk to check the cash-box. It was empty. Wherever he had gone, Matt Perry had taken the few dollars used for expenses along with him. The mayor uttered a slight curse and reached up to put out the light.

Before he could plunge the place into darkness again the door opened and a woman entered. She was small but stout, with a shiny pink face. Her breath came in gasps as though she had been hurrying.

'I've been on the look-out for you, Mayor,' she wheezed. 'He's run off. Deserted me after all these years. I'm left without a bent cent.'

Nathan held up his hand to stop the flow.

'Just a minute, Mrs Perry,' he interrupted. 'Are you telling me that Matt has left town for good?'

'That's what I'm tellin' you, Mayor,' she gasped. 'When you ordered him to go check on the Payne ranch and keep an eye out for Jack Neville, he got the shakes real bad. He's never been near the Payne spread. Each time he set off there, he just stayed away for a few days and then came back to tell you that nothin' was happening. He never went near Twin Buttes. Just spent a coupla nights on the range. He's hightailed it outa here. I'll swear he has.'

The mayor looked at her silently for a moment. His thoughts were not on her troubles but on the fact that things could have been happening of which he had no knowledge.

'Now, don't worry, Ma,' he said soothingly. 'The town will look after you, so you go home and wipe your tears. I'll sort this out.'

After a little coaxing and the handing over of

a few dollars, he got rid of the woman and went back to the saloon. The place was filling up now and he looked round for a particular person.

Wes Roberts was his nephew and the only son of the mayor's dead sister. He had taken the lad in, given him work, and prided himself on doing his Christian duty. The young man was now clearing glasses from a table as his uncle grabbed him by the arm.

'How would you like a better job, lad?' the mayor asked cheerfully. 'Something that would get you out of this place and give you some standing in the town.'

The young man looked carefully at Nathan Laird. He was a youth of middle height, broad and fair-haired. His eyes were a keen grey and there was intelligence lurking in the tanned, open countenance.

'What you got in mind, Uncle Nathan?' he asked cautiously.

'Well, now, you're a good hand with a gun, so I'm told,' the mayor said, 'and you can sure ride a horse well enough. I reckon on you making a very good marshal.'

'Marshal?' The young man nearly dropped the glasses he held in his fist. 'You got Matt Perry, Uncle Nathan.'

'He quit. Got too old and too scared for the job. So we need a younger man. One we can trust.'

The young fellow put the glasses down on the table again. His face was thoughtful and he had no illusions about his uncle's generosity.

'Don't the marshal have to be elected?' he asked.

'I've just elected you, and that's your first lesson in being a lawman. I run this town and the council does things my way. So does the marshal. That's why the pay's so good. Now, I want you to move into the jailhouse, make yourself at home there, and get a badge pinned on so that folks know we've still got some law in Coville. I'll guide you through the procedures, and I reckon on you as being the best lawman since old Eddie Faye. Are you up to it?'

'I reckon so, Uncle Nathan. But I got no horse.'

'Matt Perry's spare animal is in the corral along with his mule. You've plenty of guns in the jailhouse and your Aunt Ethel and I will supply bedding and food to start you off. Now, get rid of those glasses and go take your place in the township of Coville as its youngest and best lawman.'

# SIX

Marshal Roberts wore a new badge. He flaunted it with a certain amount of pride as he rode out of town on the first mission in his capacity as lawman of Coville. Matt Perry had taken the old badge with him and a new one was hurriedly made by the local farrier with some added enamelling by the arty schoolmarm.

Mayor Laird's orders had been quite clear: See if any fencing was being erected on the Payne spread that might block the trail to the railhead at Abilene. And also try and find out if Black Jack Neville had arrived on the scene.

The young lawman was intelligent. Maybe more so than his uncle gave him credit for. He intended to play things cautiously and had already listened to all the tales going around town. The Southern Star saloon was an ideal place for picking up the gossip, and he knew of the barbed wire and the determination of the other ranchers to do something about it.

His uncle had warned him to be on the look-out for young Allan Marwood, who might be spying out the land for his father. The new marshal knew the importance of the long valley with its water supply and short cut that did not involve rough, arid ground and a detour that added days to the journey. He rode thoughtfully towards the H bar P spread.

It was reached at mid-morning the following day and he looked from the high ground towards the sharp outlines of the twin buttes that stretched in parallel for several miles towards the north. The bright sun threw heavy shadows and the valley between the buttes was partly cast into darkness against the paleness of the stone heights.

He decided to leave his horse out of sight and go forward on foot. A rider would stand out to observers at the mouth of the valley, and Wes Roberts did not want to be seen. He left his animal contentedly grazing as he moved down the bush-littered slope towards his target. He was already on Payne land and might be challenged if any of the hands came into view and did not recognize him.

A strange vibrating noise suddenly alerted the marshal; a thudding that could not be located for a moment. He stopped to listen and shaded his eyes to peer at the distant mouth of the valley.

There were men there, and a wagon. He knew now what was happening. They were building a fence across the valley and the sound was of their hammers bedding in the posts. Wes Roberts hurried back to his horse and took the old brass telescope from his saddle-bag. He went back down the slope and lay in the waving grass to focus on what was taking place.

Joe Payne was easy to pick out. He was astride a cow pony and directing operations. His brother was on the wagon, rolling a coil of wire to the tail-board where two hands waited to carry it away.

But there was another man, and he was the one the mayor had mentioned. He was riding a large black horse along the line of the work and was tall in the saddle. His dress was entirely black and he was as thin as a beanpole. Jack Neville had arrived.

Marshal Roberts went back to his horse. He had done his job and what happened next depended upon his uncle and the local ranchers. He rode back to Coville, knowing that he would be sent off again to tell Hank Marwood or one of the others that the closing of the valley had started.

By the time he did get back to town the end of the week was bringing some of the local ranch workers into Coville for their drinks and gambling. Wes did not have to set out again. The mayor sent a message off with the hands, and within three or four days, all the spreads for miles around knew that when their cattle started moving they would hit trouble.

Hank Marwood heard about the arrival a day before the news reached Coville. His son had already scouted the valley and seen the fence being built. He had also spotted the distant figure on the black horse.

His father nodded contentedly and took down the Sharps rifle from the rack at the side of the fireplace. It was an old gun, dating back to the war and as good as the day it left the factory. The double trigger and large calibre gave it what was needed for a steady shot at long range. Hank Marwood did not intend to get close to a man with the reputation of Black Jack Neville.

He cleaned the weapon carefully under the admiring glances of his sons and the doubt in the eyes of his wife. She feared his impetuosity and had visions of ending up a widow. But with the prospect becoming more real as he checked the ammunition, she began to cheer up and savour the life of freedom that might lie ahead of her.

Hank rode out a couple of hours later, his precious rifle wrapped in a soft leather casing and with plenty of food in the saddle-bags. He rode through most of the night but rested for a few hours just before the dawn. There was no water nearby and he made do with a swig from a whiskey-bottle. A little bread and bacon satisfied his hunger, then he set out for the last few miles to Twin Buttes.

He heard the hammering and the drift of voices before he topped the final rise. It took only a moment to dismount and unpack the rifle. Hank Marwood checked the weapon before crawling to the top of the ridge and lying among the tall grass to see what was happening at the wide valley-mouth.

A cart drawn by two mules was loaded with supplies and he could see a figure standing by it who looked like young Fred Payne. Four ranch hands were working with wire and posts while another man rode quietly along the line on a black horse. Hank Marwood took a deep and slightly scared breath. The man in the saddle was tall and thin, his face shaded by a large Stetson. He was dressed completely in black.

The rancher ran an uneasy hand round the edge of his greying beard. He was beginning to sweat although the day was not yet hot. He looked around for other people or for any horses that might be saddled and ready for pursuit. It was clear that everyone had ridden on the cart and that only their protector was horsed. Hank Marwood felt a little happier. If he shot Black Jack, there would be no wild chase.

The others would be too busy ducking for cover.

He calculated the distance. Another hundred yards was needed for safety and he began to crawl down the gentle slope amid the breeze-rustled grass and bushes. There was a good position behind a tuft of thick briar and the marksman rose on one knee to set the double trigger. He wiped his eyes to get rid of the sweat and pointed the weapon at the man on horseback. It was an ideal distance, and even if the shot was not fatal Jack Neville would be out of business.

Hank Marwood gently squeezed the hair-trigger. The gun exploded as it jerked back into his shoulder with the force of the heavy charge. He was stunned for a moment by what he had done, and as the smoke cleared, he saw Black Jack tumble from his horse.

The animal trotted happily away from the fallen man and everyone around stood as though paralysed by what had happened. It took a moment to register before they all scampered for cover behind the wagon. Hank Marwood grinned happily, ran up the slope and mounted his horse. He was long gone before the men in the valley got their senses together again.

Coville lay beneath the moonlight as a mass of shadows and gentle lights issued from the many windows. Nathan Laird sat in the room above the Southern Star with his nose in a Mark Twain book that was supposed to be a good read but which only amused in parts. His wife was baking in the kitchen and seemed to be kneading the dough as though she wanted to beat it to death.

He was a bit surprised when one of the bartenders came up the stairs to tell him that Hank Marwood was down below and wanted to see him.

'Looks like he's done some hard travelling, boss,' the man opined. 'Really smelly and dusty, he is.'

'Send him up,' the mayor said as he rose from his chair.

Then he considered his wife in the other room and her sharp ear for gossip.

'I'll be down right away,' he amended hurriedly. 'Give him a drink while he's waiting.'

When he got down the broad stairs to the warmth and noise of the saloon the first person he spotted was the dusty rancher. Hank Marwood was keyed up to be a public hero. He greeted the mayor with a broad smile and raised his whiskey-glass in tribute.

'You're a long way from home, Hank,' Nathan Laird said carefully as he drew the man a little away from the other folk at the bar rail. 'Been travelling far?'

'Been hunting.'

The man glanced down at the leather-shrouded rifle that was propped against the wooden counter. The mayor looked carefully around, and when he spoke there was a certain eagerness in his voice.

'Any luck?' he asked.

'Got me a big one. The biggest in these parts. I'm figurin' that the Paynes will sing a hell of a lot smaller without their gunslinger to back 'em up.'

The mayor breathed a sigh of relief and his broad face relaxed. He signalled for more drinks.

'Does anybody know it was you did the shooting?' he asked.

'No, I got him with just one bullet and then hightailed it outa there. They all dived for cover, and I reckon that when we send our cattle through in the next few weeks nobody is goin' to start complainin' about usin' the valley.'

'I hope you're right. A range war is the last thing this town needs. The Payne lads will soon give up if the ranchers stick together and if this town gives them its support. I've got a good young marshal here now, and them hands on the Payne spread won't fight. This is the best news in weeks and I reckon a celebration is called for.'

They shared a few more whiskeys together. As the evening wore on several of their friends gathered around and Hank Marwood felt the urge to boast of his heroic deed. It was certainly heroic as he told it. He rode down the slope to the valley opening, called Jack Neville out, and they both drew at a distance of no more than a few feet. Then he rode away in triumph and the Paynes were left without their protection. The mayor listened quietly. It sounded better than the truth and the sooner word got out that Neville was dead, the quicker things could get back to normal.

Nobody paid any attention to the man who leaned on the bar at the far end of the saloon. He was tall and thin, with a face like a dried nut and a slightly amused, slightly cynical expression in his dark eyes. His white trail-coat was wrapped around him and he held a glass of beer as he listened to the animated talk.

He drained the last dregs of the cloudy liquid, pulled a wry face, and then made his way to where the little group of prominent citizens stood.

'I heard mention of Black Jack Neville,' he said politely. 'I might have got it all wrong, not bein' an educated fella like you gents, but what's all this about shootin' him?'

One of the local storekeepers pointed at Hank Marwood.

'This is the fella had a shoot-out with Neville,' he said proudly. 'Stopped a range war and saved this town from losin' one hell of a lotta business.'

'Is that a fact now?' The stranger shook his head in bewilderment. 'And all this happened out at Twin Buttes?'

Hank Marwood nodded.

'Right at the entrance to the valley,' he said proudly.

'Well, ain't that somethin' to think about?' the man said admiringly. 'Just one little problem though. Jack Neville ain't never been to Twin Buttes. He decided to stop off in Coville for the night and take a drink in this saloon.'

He flung open the trail-coat and disclosed the dark shirt and black pants. There were two guns at his waist and he tucked the edges of the trail-coat behind the holsters.

'I think you'd better change your story, fella,' he said smoothly, 'because I ain't too happy with the one you're puttin' about now.'

The folk around Hank Marwood suddenly found that he needed more space. They all retreated to a safe distance. They were led by the mayor who was standing at the bottom of the stairs before anyone else really began to move.

'It's just you and me, fella,' Jack Neville said in his silky voice. 'You got a gun, so draw when you're ready. Maybe you'll be tellin' folk the truth after all. If you're real lucky.'

Hank Marwood licked his lips. He wanted to run away but they were all watching him. He was caught by his own boasting and he reached down for the pistol at his belt.

There was a single shot and the rancher staggered back against the bar. The gun fell from his limp grip and he bent over as though in an effort to pick it up again. His left hand grabbed the counter for support as he slipped face down on the sawdusted floor.

'Get the marshal!' somebody yelled.

'No!'

The mayor used the power of his official voice to stem any movement towards the door.

'It was a fair fight and we just need the mortician,' he said.

He walked sedately towards the stranger and motioned him to put his gun away.

'He talked too much,' he said in as calm a voice as he could muster. 'Drunks let their imaginations run off now and then. They're not very responsible people. You mustn't judge Coville by one man.'

He took the gunman by the arm and led him to a corner of the room.

'If you have not taken employment locally, there is a job on offer in our little community.'

'I gotta job.'

'Ah, with the Paynes?'

The man nodded and the mayor shook his head dolefully.

'Then their gain is our loss,' he confessed sadly.

# SEVEN

Marshal Roberts rode slowly towards the Payne ranch. He had a lot on his mind and the message he was carrying from the mayor did not help. He had never fired a gun in anger; had never killed anybody, and had never been shot at. He could shoot. There was no doubt about that. And he was quick on the draw. But that did not make a real lawman. This was his first trial.

A week or more had gone by since Black Jack Neville had left town to take up employment with the Paynes. Cattle would soon be on the move to the Abilene railhead, and then the trouble would start on a big scale. The ranchers were subdued for the time being. The death of Hank Marwood had scared them, and there had even been tales of some of their hands quitting before the killing started to involve them.

He topped the ridge and the long valley came into sight. There did not seem to be any activity down there and the whole place appeared to be deserted. The wire fence was not clear at first. The early rains had dulled the wire and the posts were surrounded by tall bushes and grass. But it was there all right, and as he neared the wide entrance between the dark buttes he could see the large gap through which a herd of animals could be driven without any problems at all.

Wes began to think that work must have stopped and the whole plan called off. He rode quietly through the gap and reined in his horse to look around for guards. Nothing stirred and the marshal rode on towards the ranch house, which was still several miles away.

The large building looked deserted at first glance, but as Wes drew up at the hitching-rail, the door opened and Betty Payne stood on the veranda with a welcoming smile on her face. She had known Wes Roberts since they were kids together, learning from the Blue Back speller under the tyranny of the schoolmarm in Coville.

'Well, if you ain't the welcomest stranger I've seen for a long time.' She smiled as he hitched the horse and shook the dust from his clothes.

'You're lookin' well, Betty. Bein' married seems to suit you.' Wes grinned back as she led him into the house. 'Is Joe around?'

'Somewheres up near the creek, I figure, but he'll he back for the midday meal. And I reckon you'll be puttin' your feet under the table with us.'

'Sure will if you cook as good as your ma did.'

She waved him to a chair and went to the stove where the hot coffee-pot was ready. He sipped the strong brew gratefully and looked round the large and sweet-smelling room.

'Where's Fred?' he asked as she sat down opposite him.

'He's off on the trail with a herd for Abilene,' she said. 'They set off two days ago to beat the rush.'

'And what about your new fella, Jack Neville?'

She smiled slightly.

'You passed him on the way here,' she said. 'He's up on the buttes with a few men. They see everything that goes on in the valley. That's what he's paid for.'

'That figures. So a lone rider or a small group would be let through, but a herd of cattle. . . ?'

She nodded.

'You got it, Wes. No cattle go through that valley until Fred has a few days' start on them.'

'Then you do intend to let folks use the valley after all?' Wes asked. 'That makes more sense than havin' a range war. I'm glad to hear it.'

She shook her head.

'It's not quite like that, Wes,' she said firmly. 'The lads were goin' to cut off the valley completely at first. But after them two killings they decided to play it different. The cattle can go through at a few cents a head.'

There was a long silence before the lawman put his cup down on the table.

'Joe and Fred is surely playin' with fire,' he mused. 'The neighbours are not goin' to like that any more than havin' to take the long route. There'll be more killings, Betty. Can't you make them see sense?'

'Cattle prices depend on first come, first sold,' she said bluntly. 'Old Harry was never happy about the damage done to the grazin' on our land. But he put up with it. Them ranchers had pioneered alongside him. But the lads are young and it's their future. That valley is bein' over-grazed and we've had to send our own animals further out on the range. You know how much more work goes into roundin' them up again.'

'Is it worth folk bein' killed?'

'You and me might think not, but we're not ranchers, Wes.'

'Who was the fella that Hank Marwood shot?'

She sighed. 'That was Joe's idea,' she said. 'He hired a hobo to dress in black and ride up and down the valley entrance while the hands were workin' on the fence. He knew that if anybody saw him, they'd think it was Black Jack and be scared to hell. It was a damn-fool idea, I reckon. But the damage is done now and we buried him decent.'

'That'll be a comfort to him. Tell me, Betty, have you heard about Alex Smith bein' killed?'

He was watching the woman carefully as he spoke but her look seemed to be one of genuine suprise.

'No, I hadn't heard. Where did this happen?'

'Oh, he'd been out for a night in some small township near their spread. Somebody bushwhacked him.'

'Well, it don't concern us.'

'No, but if the other two Smith brothers think that Joe and Fred are gettin' even, it might cause some trouble. Don't you reckon so?'

She blinked as she considered the matter for a few moments.

'Fred and Joe ain't left here for weeks,' she said slowly. 'All the hands can vouch for that.'

'I wasn't suggestin' they killed him,' Wes said quietly. 'It's what the Smiths think that matters. They could join forces with the local ranchers, couldn't they?'

'Why should they? They're way up north. Abilene is on their doorstep.'

'Just to make trouble, Betty. When folk start killin' each other, it sorta gets outa hand.'

'I guess you're right. Is that what you came here to tell us?'

'Not quite. I got business with Joe, and it's what you might call official. He ain't gonna like it one little bit.'

Betty Payne glanced at the new clock and then took a look through the window.

'Joe should be back any time now,' she said nervously. 'He's not one to miss a meal. I'd better start puttin' it on the table.'

'Where are the kids?'

'They're out with old Steve on their ponies. Gettin' right good with them, they are.'

The voice was more cheerful for a moment and then her face saddened again.

'I don't like this any more than you do, Wes,' she murmured. 'But what can we do?'

Joe arrived a few minutes later and greeted Wes Roberts with a certain reserve. They knew each other but were not old friends. Joe seldom went into town and had never regarded Wes as being more than a young lad who brushed out the saloon and helped behind the bar.

'So, what brings you out here, Wes?' he asked as they sat down to eat.

'It's about your pa, Joe,' the marshal said carefully. 'I've been sent by Judge Crawford and Lawyer Mason with some papers they say I gotta serve on you.'

Joe put down his knife and fork to stare at the embarrassed young man.

'That sure as hell sounds like some legal turkey-gobbling lawyer,' he said with an attempt at lightness. 'Have I been misbehaving?'

'No, no, Joe. Nothin' like that. It's about your late pa, as I said. He had a wife, Joe. And she owns a share of this spread.'

70

\*

Things quietened down again in about an hour and Wes Roberts was able to state the case for the judge and the lawyer in a calmer atmosphere.

'Your pa wasn't just makin' up to the widow Jones,' he explained carefully to a red-faced Joe. 'He actually married her before a preacher and a judge. There are witnesses, documents, and there's even a will your pa drew up. He leaves a half-share of this ranch to her durin' her lifetime, and you and Fred inherit after her death. She drew up a similar will. Her spread goes to your pa if she dies first. It was all square and legal.'

'That's one hell of a thing to do to us. Can we claim that pa was as mad as a fightin' bull? He's sure acted like it.'

Wes shook his head doubtfully.

'Her lawyer is in town now,' he said. 'He's presented her claim to Judge Crawford and the judge had a word with Lawyer Mason. They can't find a fault in it. That's the law, Joe. You and Fred is workin' with your new stepmother as a partner.'

Betty put a consoling hand on Joe's shoulder.

'So that's why the Smith brothers wanted to kill Pa,' she said. 'They'd heard that he'd married their sister and they figured on our

71

family gettin' her spread?'

'Yes, I reckon so, but with Mr Payne dying first, her land is safe for her brothers and she's got a share in this place.'

Joe got up from his chair and walked over to the window. He stared out bleakly at the oncoming dusk.

'I wish to hell Pa was here. He'd have known what to do,' he said miserably.

'He's dead,' Betty snapped. 'Don't forget that, Joe. Your pa is dead.'

# EIGHT

Ned Smith was alone for the first time in a week. He stood by the cattle-pens and watched his ranch hands go off noisily to spend the money he had just paid them. The drive was over; the Smith animals were safely at the railhead, and there could be a few days of drinking and roistering before the trek back to the ranch.

The air was filled with the smell of the cattle. There was a haze of smoke coming from the nearby locomotive, which was getting up a head of steam ready for the journey East. The sun was going down and Abilene was a very different town from what it had been the last time the Smith brothers visited.

There were only two of them now. Alex had been shot up in some quarrel or other and Abie was back looking after the spread. It had all been left to one-eyed Ned, and he felt proud of the deals he had made. He looked round the busy pens with a sigh of satisfaction before mounting his horse and crossing the railtracks to the other side of town. He needed to quench his thirst, and then he fancied a trip to Cedar Street where all the action took place.

He was carrying a gun, but it was hidden away. Abilene still had rules about firearms and he had no wish to break the law when his brothers were not there to back him. But Ned was not looking for trouble. The drive had been successful and he was at peace with the world. The idea of a warrant against the Smiths for the Payne killing had been forgotten. They were too important to the commerce of the town. And had the money to smooth things over with the right people.

He was so content with life that he did not notice the old man who had been tailing him ever since the Smith cattle hit town. The scruffy old fellow had been waiting for them and had carefully followed Ned Smith everywhere he went. He followed him now, a bent figure on an aged mule. He did not appear to carry a gun but, like Ned, he kept it well hidden.

It was a long night as Harry Payne's victim moved from saloon to saloon. He kept clear of his own ranch hands and enjoyed the company of flashily dressed girls on occasions. The man was throwing money around, and by the time he decided to call it a night, he was rolling slightly and had trouble mounting his horse. He steered it clumsily towards the edge of town where camp had been made when the herd entered Abilene. There were two large canvas tents, a smaller one for him, and a chuck wagon. An elderly cook was now slumbering gently in front of a dying fire.

Ned unsaddled his horse, tethered it to the line with the others, and crossed to the fire to see if there was some refreshing coffee to be had. He filled a tin cup, drank some of the over-stewed stuff, and threw the rest away.

He ignored the snoring cook and staggered across to the smaller tent. It was a struggle to light the oil-lamp that dangled from the centre pole and he swore as he did it. He cast off his hat and boots and was just about to settle down when something made him turn round. A figure stood outlined at the open flap of the tent. It was the ragged old man.

'Who – who the hell are you?' Ned asked without any great interest.

'Harry Payne.'

The words did not register for a moment and the rancher peered at the figure with his one good eye.

'Payne?' he whispered. 'Payne?'

'Yeah. The fella you and your brothers shot in this town a few months back. Forgotten already, Ned?'

Ned Smith swayed as he stared at the apparition before him. Moths were beginning to gather round the oil-lamp and one settled on the sweating face.

'That can't be, fella,' he said as he waved an uncertain hand at the insect. 'Abie killed old Harry Payne well and truly. Right there on the street. All the folks saw it and we had to get outa town fast.'

Harry smiled and shook his head.

'I already killed Alex,' he said softly, 'and you got a gun under your coat. Just like I have. So use it, fella.'

Ned Smith made a move with his right hand. He grasped the butt of the gun and yanked it from inside his coat. It caught on a stuffed wallet and that came out as well. It flooded the ground with the money that had just been paid for the cattle sales.

Harry responded to the move like lightning. His gun was out and cocked almost before the wallet hit the earth. The shot made the lamp vibrate and Ned Smith reeled back. He dropped his own weapon and nearly collapsed the little tent as he fell to the ground. Harry stood for a moment, watching the body twitch amid the beetles that crawled over the sandy gravel.

He was just putting the gun away when another figure burst into the tent.

It was the elderly cook. He had woken from a drunken sleep and came charging along with a shotgun that was pushed before him like a battering ram.

'I gotcha, fella!' he shouted as he raised the weapon to fire.

Harry beat him to it and pulled the trigger of the Colt. The man staggered backwards out of the opening and the shotgun blasted into the night air as the old cook reeled off a few paces before collapsing.

There was a silence which was only broken by the hum of insects as Harry looked round the camping-site. There was nobody else about and the outskirts of the town were at least a hundred yards away. He picked up the fallen wallet and the spilled banknotes with a wry grin on his face. They were placed safely inside his shirt before he went out to the darkness of the night.

His mule was waiting patiently some distance away and bore him back to a hitching-rail by the cattle-pens. His own horse was tethered there and he switched animals. The mule had been rented locally and the owner could collect it in the morning.

Harry Payne rode off towards the south, whistling happily as he contemplated a future with only one more Smith brother to kill.

# NINE

Joe and Fred Payne were making money, but they were worried men. They now had a co-owner of the ranch unless they could contact Harry and sort out the whole business. It had never occured to them that the old fool would actually marry the woman and make a mess of everything by exchanging wills.

Joe had already sent the arranged message to his father through the bank. He had added ten dollars to the monthly sum he paid to the account of Bill Dean and hoped it would bring Harry home quickly. It also occured to him that neither he nor Fred actually knew where Uncle Jesse's place was. If Harry did not go to the bank that month to collect his money everything would be delayed and the widow Jones would be arriving to take her share of the ranch profits. Both lads also feared that she might bring one or two of her brothers with her.

The Payne cattle had gone to the railhead and arrived nearly a week before their neighbours could reach Abilene. There had nearly been bloodshed at the entrance to the valley, but the few extra men whom Joe had hired and the brooding sight of Black Jack Neville up on the butte had been enough to calm things down.

The local ranchers paid the few cents a head unwillingly. They threatened among themselves to kill the Paynes once their hired gun departed.

They complained to the mayor of Coville, but there was nothing more he could do. Even the judge could not fault the reasoning of the Payne brothers. Trouble flared in the town when the ranch hands came in at the weekends for their spending-spree. The new marshal had his first bit of bother when Elijah Bowen's foreman picked a fight with one of the Payne hands.

Wes Roberts was called from the jailhouse and approached the saloon fearfully and with a shotgun under his arm. He heard firing before he reached the brightly lit place, but when he entered through the swing-doors things were not quite what he expected.

The two quarrelling men had been too drunk to shoot straight. An oil-lamp was shattered, one of the windows had a hole through it, and Elijah Bowen's foreman was being held upright by his friends. Wes soon cleared them out of the saloon and local folks regarded him as a hero from that time on.

And the hero now sat in the mayor's office where a few select members of the council were discussing the situation. Takings had dropped off in the saloons after the shooting. The Paynes no longer came into town for supplies, and economic reality had raised its ugly head. So something had to be done about it.

The councilmen wrangled aimlessly while they smoked and drank at the mayor's expense. Their pointless discussions were only ended when a knock at the door heralded the arrival of the telegraph clerk. He was a small man with long, straight hair and twitching eyes which now peered owlishly at the mayor.

'I thought you'd like to know right away,' he said urgently, 'but an important rancher's been killed in Abilene. Fella called Ned Smith.'

The councilmen looked at each other and there was a moment of silence.

'Wasn't his brother killed a few weeks back?' one of the storekeepers asked.

Nathan Laird nodded.

'That's right,' he said in a slightly puzzled voice. 'Shot on his way home from a visit to a local town. And they're the brothers of Ma Jones, who was married to old Harry Payne.'

'Now, ain't that a strange thing?' the judge wheezed. 'Them Smith brothers ain't married, so she and the last fella got themselves the Smith spread between them. That Ma Jones is surely one rich woman by now.'

'And a widow,' the banker laughed. 'Twice over.'

The mayor tapped the table-top thoughtfully.

'So she owns her own ranch, part of the spread that belonged to her brothers, and she's got a share of the Payne lands. That surely sounds like good fortune shining down on her. I wonder if somebody is giving it a helping hand.'

The meeting broke up shortly afterwards without having done anything useful. The marshal waited to be dismissed and the banker also lingered until the door was closed behind the other departing councilmen.

Will Fortnum was a shrewd man and sat down again as though ready to impart something of importance. The mayor poured another drink for each of them and he and the marshal waited for the revelation.

'You'll recall that the two Payne lads were paying a sum of money into the account of a fellow called Bill Dean every month?' the banker began.

They nodded in unison and Will Fortnum leaned across the table earnestly.

'Well, I was wrong about it being for Black Jack Neville. He's at their ranch now but that money is still being paid out. Every month. What

81

do you make of that?'

Wes Roberts kept his mouth shut. He knew that no answer was expected from him. It was the mayor who must reply.

'We're being bamboozled,' Nathan Laird said slowly. 'The Paynes are doing something I just don't understand. Let's think about this. Harry went and married that widow woman and they made wills in favour of each other. So now she gets half his ranch. As the Smith brothers die off, she also gets more of their spread as her family share. So, is Joe Payne behind all this?'

The banker thought about it for a moment.

'I don't see how,' he said. 'Neither Joe nor Fred has left the ranch since the cattle-drive to Abilene. Fred made that trip in plenty of company. And it can't be Black Jack who's doing the killings. He's stuck at the H bar P collecting the money for using the valley route. And there's one other odd thing. They paid out an extra ten dollars this month.'

The mayor rubbed his chin thoughtfully.

'If the last Smith brother dies now,' he said, 'the widow-woman would have all their spread plus her share of the Payne land. And on top of that, there's what she inherited from her first husband. But suppose she died? What then?'

'Unless she made a new will, I reckon the Paynes would have the lot.'

It was young Wes Roberts who said it without

thinking of his minor place in society.

'You're right, lad,' the mayor said cheerfully. 'And that's the game the Paynes are playing. Those two young hellions aim to control the biggest spread for a couple of hundred miles around. So how do we stop them?'

'Do we need to?' Will Fortnum asked shrewdly.

The moneylender's mind was working out the financial prospects. And the Payne family were his customers. He could foresee a golden future for the bank in Coville. There was a long silence as the First Citizen contemplated the matter.

'It needs thinking about,' he conceded. 'We mustn't go off half-cock on this thing. I reckon that this fellow they're paying money to each month could be a hired gun. He's the one killing off the Smiths.'

He looked at the young marshal.

'I got a job for you, Wes. I want you to track down this Bill Dean and find out why he's being paid this money. He has to call in to that bank in – where is it, Will?'

'A little township called Watona up by those old gold-workings along the river.'

'Yes. Well, go there, young Wes, and see what you can find out. Coville's quiet enough and it won't take you more than a week or so.'

The marshal hesitated for a moment.

'I gotta question, Uncle Nathan,' he said.

'Well, spit it out, boy.'

'Mr Fortnum said that the Paynes put an extra ten dollars into Dean's account this month. Who came into town with the message?'

The mayor looked approvingly at his nephew. It was something that had not occured to him. The banker answered easily.

'It was Fred's wife,' he said. 'She's the only Payne who's been into Coville since this trouble started.'

'Does it matter?' the mayor asked.

Wes Roberts shrugged.

'I was sorta wonderin' if it was to be paid every month or just this month,' he said.

'The boy's got a point,' Will Fortnum mused. 'She told the clerk that it was only for one month. But does it mean anything?'

'Could be a bonus for another killing,' Wes told him.

Watona township was just about as small as you could get and yet still have a bank. It also possessed a schoolhouse, and a marshal sitting in a rocking-chair on the stoop of his office.

Jim Brady was a big man with several days' growth of beard. His eyes were narrowed as he peered at the horseman coming down the street. The rider was young and a stranger, and as he got nearer the marshal saw something he did not expect to see. The young fellow was a lawman and his badge was still new and shiny. The marshal grinned and spat at a passing roach. He was even more surprised when the stranger reined in at the jailhouse and dismounted.

'Well, they surely is makin' marshallin' a job for young fellas in some parts,' Jim Brady growled. 'Where you from, boy?'

Wes Roberts kept his temper and stood with one hand on the head of his horse.

'Coville,' he said quietly.

'That's one hell of a journey. I take it that you got some business here in town.'

'Yes, Marshal. I'm lookin' for a man by the name of Dean. Bill Dean. Know him?'

The marshal's eyes flickered a little although there was no change in his facial expression.

'We ain't got nobody in town by that name,' he said slowly. 'What would you be wantin' him for?'

'I don't know that we do want him, but he may be able to help us with a few problems we got back in Coville.'

The local lawman sat up in his chair and it creaked under the shifting weight.

'I heard tell that them Payne fellas is causing trouble round there,' he said. 'Got anythin' to do with that?'

'Could have. He seems to be on their pay-roll.'

That seemed to bring Jim Brady to life.

'Is that a fact now?' he exclaimed before he could restrain himself. 'Well – I don't know the fella.'

'I'll ask round town then. Somebody might have come across him.'

'No.'

The marshal stood up and placed one hand firmly on the gun at his side. He leaned forward over the hitching-rail until his dark face was inches away from that of young Wes Roberts.

'I reckon it's best you leave town, fella,' he said with grim emphasis. 'Folks round here are mostly kin to each other and don't like strangers askin' questions. Just get back on that horse of your'n and ride out while you still can. I don't want no killings in my town.'

Several people were within hearing by now and they stood unashamedly listening to the exchange. The looks they gave their marshal were not those of support, and one old man was grinning at his discomfiture.

'That sounds as if you don't keep a very law-abidin' town, Marshal,' Wes said with a calm he was not feeling. 'I'll just pay a call on the bank if you've got no objections.'

'I got objections. I told you to get the hell out.'

The man's angry voice was raised enough to alert the whole street, and everyone had stopped to watch what was happening. Wes decided to back off. He said nothing but got on his horse and swung the animal round the way he had come. Jim Brady stood triumphantly watching him ride up the street. He turned to the folk around with a broad grin on his face.

'We don't let no strangers tell us how to run things in this town,' he boasted.

The crowd just looked at him with hate in their eyes, and he waved a dismissive hand before going into his office. He did not see the grinning old man run after Wes Roberts and catch him up just outside the bank.

'Marshal,' he called breathlessly, 'I got a few words to say to you, but take yourself off the main street and wait for me by the corral behind the saloon.'

Wes nodded and turned down the small alley to where an array of corrals stretched along parallel to the main street. He dismounted again and stood waiting for the appearance of the old-timer.

The man came hurrying out of another side lane a few moments later. He looked around carefully before approaching Wes and then came across to where the marshal stood by his horse.

'I don't mind most folks seein' us together, Marshal,' he said, 'but I don't reckon to gettin' on the bad side of Jim Brady. From what I heard back there, you're lookin' for Bill Dean?'

'That's right. You know him?'

'As well as most folks do, I figure. He don't come to town very often and he don't go drinkin' in the saloon much, or anythin' like that. Quiet sorta fella, is Bill Dean.'

'A gunslinger?'

The old man blinked his watering eyes.

'Bless you, no,' he chuckled. 'No more than most of us unless we're pushed to it. But I don't see old Billy Dean goin' round lookin' for trouble.'

'Old!' Wes Roberts looked hard at the man. 'You mean that this Bill Dean is not a young fella on the prod?'

He got a vigorous shake of the head by way of reply.

'Hell, no. He's damned near as old as I am, son. Limps along like he's all rheumaticky.'

Wes pondered the situation for a moment or two while the flies buzzed around and the old fellow watched with one hand slightly outstretched. The marshal took the hint and slipped a dollar into the grubby palm.

'And where will I find him?' he asked.

The old man pointed to the west and gave a pretty good description of the route to where Bill Dean lived. It was a journey of nearly half a day and the young marshal thanked him before remounting and getting ready to head in that direction. One more thought occured to him.

'Has he been into town lately?' he asked.

Another shake of the head.

'No, not since last month when he just had one drink in the saloon, made a call at the bank, and bought a few supplies. Ain't seen him since.'

Wes nodded his thanks and turned his horse to ride off.

It was at that moment that the town marshal came tearing round the corner from the main street. Some interfering person had called into the jailhouse to tell him that the stranger was talking to the old man.

Wes Roberts was twenty yards or so away by then but turned when he heard the raucous shout the marshal gave on seeing that the two had been meeting and talking. Jim Brady grabbed the old man by the collar and pushed him back against the rails of a corral. Then his large hand smashed into the man's face, backwards and forwards in vicious slaps.

Wes Roberts swung his horse back again and rode to where the lawman was still slapping his victim about.

'You sure is one brave fella,' Wes Roberts said quietly. His voice was steady, but for the first time in his life, he was facing a professional gun in a strange town.

Jim Brady turned in surprise and pushed the old man against the corral as he switched his attention to a new opponent.

'I told you not to go round askin' questions in this town, fella,' he shouted at Wes. 'This old fool has a loose tongue and I don't aim he should go gabbin' to the likes of you. Now, get the hell outa here before I drag you off that flea-bitten nag and give you some of the same.'

A few people were beginning to gather at a discreet distance and one elderly woman had the courage to run over to the old man and help him move further away.

'You won't do that, Marshal,' Wes said firmly. 'I ain't an old man and I'm carryin' a gun.'

Jim Brady's glare wavered for a moment. He was used to having people back off when he threatened, but now it was different. Folk were watching and his reputation was at stake. He stifled a curse and reached down for the gun at his waist. Both men drew at about the same time but Wes had used an old trick taught him by an ex-soldier. He had already pulled back the hammer, and when he fired, his shot was as accurate as he could have wished.

It caught the marshal full in the chest and the man stood for a moment with surprise on his face. He half-raised his own gun but it wavered as he pitched forward and lay still.

Wes looked around the gathering crowd. If he expected hostility, there was none. Some of the faces even showed a certain delight at the sight of the dead lawman. Wes Roberts turned his horse and rode out of town. Nobody bothered to pursue him.

He took the route the old man had laid out for him. It was a poor trail and he stopped at a brackish creek for a rest and something to eat. The small place he was heading for was a few patches of grazing, some cultivated land, and a couple of dozen hogs wandering around amid a small herd of milk-cows. The house was of adobe and with smoke coming out of an iron stovepipe.

Wes tethered his horse out of sight and took out the old brass telescope. He lay on his stomach to watch the place until he saw who was living there.

After he had satisfied himself on that point, the marshal rode back to Watona. He visited the bank, asked a few questions around town, turned down the job of marshal, but had a drink in the saloon.

# TEN

It was peaceful and quiet in Coville, but Nathan Laird was a worried man. The cattle-runs had ended and the local ranchers were having meetings to decide what to do about the Paynes. The ranch hands had not been near town to spend their wages, and neither the saloons nor the stores were doing much in the way of business. Even the bank was complaining about how quiet things were, and it was that quietness that had the mayor worried.

He could sense that something was in the wind, and was thankful to see young Wes Roberts back in town. The marshal reported to the mayoral office after he had cleaned up and eaten. He told his story in simple terms and Nathan Laird listened avidly.

'And so this fellow wasn't at home then?' the First Citizen mused. 'And he's an elderly man? It don't make sense, Wes. And why was the town

92

marshal so uppity about you asking questions? None of it sounds right. Have you got any ideas, lad?'

Wes hesitated.

'It's only a guess, Uncle Nathan,' he said slowly, 'but the man I spoke to said that Bill Dean walked with a limp. All sorta rheumaticky was how he described it.'

'So?'

'Harry Payne walked with a limp.'

'But . . .' The mayor's eyes flickered as he thought about it. 'Yes, that's a good point you have there, lad. Could the old devil still be alive? Somebody was shot in Abilene, but suppose we've all been fooled and Harry Payne is going around killing off the Smith brothers so that his wife inherits their land. She could be in it with him.'

'What about his sons?'

'I don't know, but my guess is that they have to be involved as well. The Payne family could be planning the biggest land grab we've ever seen in these parts. It's just the sort of thing old Harry *would* think up. So what do we do about it?'

Wes Roberts looked down at his empty glass.

'You're mayor of Coville, Uncle Nathan, and I'm town marshal. We don't have no powers outside this place. It's up to the local ranchers and the county sheriff.'

'You could be right, boy, but I've got a feeling

that something is brewing out there. The week-end's on us and the town is empty. You could ride over to the Payne spread and see what's going on. I'd certainly like to know whether or not Black Jack is still around.'

That was what Wes Roberts had feared.

'I got no authority out there, Uncle Nathan,' he said, 'and I ain't no match for a fella like Black Jack. I got lucky with that marshal at Watona, but Jack Neville's a different nest of rattlers.'

'I'm not suggesting you go looking for trouble, lad. Just see if that fence is still there and if the valley is being guarded. After all, the drives are over for the season, and Black Jack might have gone on his way. He'd be an expensive man to hire all the year round. I also hear tell that the Paynes took on a few other extra hands. They can't pay them once the season is over. It would-n't make sense. Just watch your step is all.'

'I'll sure as hell do that.'

'Good. Then set out in the morning.'

Wes Roberts was already too late. The ranchers had met at the Double W spread to decide what action to take. They could muster nearly forty men between them and their smaller neigh-bours. A move had been worked out and a strong force of riders was already heading for the entrance to the valley.

They had started out before dawn and the sun was strong and high in the sky when the two buttes were sighted. There was no sign of activity but a small plume of smoke wavered up into the haze from a grassy ridge. It showed that somebody was on guard, looking down on the entrance to the valley and alert for any intruders.

There were some twenty or more riders approaching the long row of posts that carried the rusting barbed wire. They did not make for the wide gap that would have let them pass into the valley. They spread out along the fencing while ropes were produced from the pommels of their horses. They tied the ends of the ropes to the strong posts, and at a given signal from Elijah Bowen, began to pull them from the ground.

Some of the men were whooping at the sheer pleasure of beating the Payne family. The posts began to rip from their positions and the loosened wire sprang up in jagged arcs that the horsemen had to avoid.

A shot rang out and one of the riders toppled to the ground while his mount galloped off, dragging a wooden post and a trail of barbed wire.

Everyone stopped what they were doing and all eyes turned to where a thin man stood on a ridge with a rifle tucked under his arm. He was dressed in black and his dark face was partly hidden by a black Stetson. Jack Neville was still around.

Elijah Bowen sensed that the fight was going out of the men. He drew the Winchester from its saddle holster and steadied his mount as he levelled the weapon at the silent figure on the ridge. Wally Williams was at his side and put a restraining hand on the rancher's arm.

'This could get kinda messy, Elijah,' he said. 'That fella ain't likely to be alone up there and our men won't stand and fight. They're not gunslingers, for God's sake. Look at them now.'

Elijah Bowen shook him off angrily.

'This is our only chance to finish it once and for all,' he snapped. 'If I can pick off that killin' bastard, our fellas will support us. And don't forget, we have other irons in the fire right now.'

He raised the rifle but the target had vanished from sight. They all looked up at the reddish rocks but nothing stirred. The smoke from a camp-fire still rose faintly into the sky and a few birds were settling again after the shooting. The ranch hands were quiet now. They huddled together and their horses seemed to be moving further away from the entrance to the valley. The men looked to their bosses uncertainly and few of them seemed anxious to get involved with a professional killer.

Elijah Bowen turned to face them and his

stubby, tough body gave the only sign of real leadership.

'Get your Winchesters out!' he shouted at them, 'and aim up at them ridges. If anythin' moves, shoot the hell out of it. We're takin' all this fencin' down and no hired gun is gonna stop us.'

The men drew their carbines and looked up at the ridges along the twin buttes with uncertain expressions on their faces. Elijah Bowen pointed to two of the tougher-looking hands.

'You, Matt, and you, Harvey, get your ropes round the rest of these fence posts and start pullin' them out,' he ordered. 'The rest of us will keep you covered.'

The two men looked at each other and one of them had the courage to shake his head.

'Hank Warren's already dead, Mr Bowen,' he said firmly. 'I don't reckon to end up like that for the sake of a few dollars. No disrespect, but I'm a cowpoke, not a lawman.'

Elijah Bowen snorted his anger and rode over to the man. He grabbed the rope from an unprotesting hand and turned his horse back to the fencing. It took only a moment to tie the lasso to one of the posts and he was ready to tear the wooden support from the ground.

The shot took him in the upper chest and the startled rancher still held the rope for a moment before pitching to the ground and rolling over a few times. All the ranch hands galloped madly out of range and even Wally Williams and the scrawny Hugh Evans realized that it was time to beat a retreat.

They galloped their horses after the fleeing ranch hands, then the whole group stopped at a safe distance and watched the buttes for signs of life. One of the men noticed that Elijah Bowen was still moving a little; he spurred his horse forward slowly as he raised one hand in the air to convey the message that he was not bent on causing trouble.

While his companions watched, he got down and knelt over the stricken rancher.

'He's still alive!' he shouted. 'Bring a horse over here.'

Elijah's own animal had by now joined the others. One of the hands took up its reins and went out to help. The two men hoisted their wounded boss over the saddle and got him back to the group.

'Take him straight into Coville,' Wally Williams told them, with an attempt at recovering his authority. 'Maybe Doc Hawson can help him.'

The two men nodded and set off thankfully for safer parts.

'So what do we do now?' Hugh Evans asked in his dry, gravelly voice.

'We wait,' Wally Williams told him. 'We do what we planned to do at the start. We just sit tight and wait.'

The men got down from their horses and built a couple of fires to make some coffee. The atmosphere became more relaxed, and while one man kept watch on the valley entrance, the rest lounged around and drank the hot brew while they talked uneasily among themselves. The two ranchers sat side by side, mugs in their hands, and their faces set and anxious.

It was a couple of hours before anything happened. Then they heard a series of shots and Wally Williams let out a whoop of delight.

'They got here!' he shouted. 'Get to horse and let's go clear them fellas out of the valley.'

The hands showed little enthusiasm but they obeyed. The group was soon galloping towards the line of damaged fencing again. Men were moving now among the ridges high in the buttes. They seemed to be leaving what had been good hiding-places to retreat from the oncoming horsemen.

Wally Williams had worked it out carefully and his plan was coming off at last. Five days ago he had sent another group of riders under the command of his son, to bypass the valley and come into it from the northern end at a prearranged time.

They were now careering through the wide, watered space and the few men who had been guarding the entrance were trapped. The hands sensed that they were now on the winning side and they began to holler and whoop as they goaded their mounts past the fencing and over the lush grass that the Payne family had been charging their bosses to cross.

It was soon over. The two groups of invaders had closed the line of retreat and the few defenders who scrambled down to level ground found that they could not reach their horses. There were five of them and they stood despondently in a group as the excited ranch hands circled them, their mounts threatening to ride them down. Wally Williams stopped it by raising a commanding hand.

'You fellas was just doin' your job,' he said bluntly, 'and we ain't got no quarrel with that. But now you all get the hell outa here. And go south. You don't return to the Payne spread, and if any of you try it, we'll sure as hell kill you.'

'What about our horses?' one of the men was brave enough to ask.

'We ain't roundin' them up in the middle of all this hoo-ha. And I figure on how they belong to the Paynes anyhows. You just start walkin' for Coville or points south. And remember, if we come up against you again, there ain't gonna be no second chance.'

He turned to look around the valley and the distant northern gap beyond which the Payne house lay.

'Where the hell is that fella Neville?' he asked nobody in particular.

There was no sign of the man in black. He had vanished from sight. The professional gun had been high on the ridges and been first to spot the horsemen coming through the valley from the north. He knew that the game was up before anybody else realized it. And Black Jack did what every good mercenary does when the chips are down. He quietly retired to a spot among the rocks which he had already chosen for emergencies. It was an overhang partly shielded by scrub, and all he had to do was to stay there until everybody had left. He had lost his horse, but saved his life. And that was what mattered.

Wally Williams was now in command of the situation. He led the way triumphantly along the valley to the north. The horses of the defeated men accompanied him and he was headed towards the Payne ranch house for a show-down.

The place was quiet when they arrived. There were no horses at the hitching-rails, and no smoke from the stovepipes. The other adjoining buildings seemed closed up and deserted. Wally Williams raised a hand to halt his men and they sat their horses for a moment, waiting for what must happen next.

It was almost as though a climax was past and there was nothing more to be done. Wally raised himself in the saddle and shouted.

'Hey, you in there! We're here to tell you that there ain't no more fencin' and that the valley is free to all decent folk. So come out and face your neighbours, Joe Payne. Make your peace while you still can.'

There was a slight noise somewhere to his left and the rancher swung round to see the shutters open on one of the large bunkhouses. A shotgun poked through, and before he could do anything, both barrels let fly.

Other windows and doors flew open. There was a hail of lead from all three sides and the invading horsemen were caught in a murderous fire that brought men and horses down in writhing masses. Wally Williams took buckshot in his right shoulder and arm. His mount reared as its flank was peppered. He swore mightily and headed for open space, regardless of anything but saving himself.

The others were doing the same thing. They galloped madly from the scene, leaving the fallen to look after themselves. The invasion of the Payne ranch was over as the horsemen scattered to rush back the way they had come.

The door of the bunkhouse opened after a brief silence. One of the ranch hands emerged with a shotgun at the ready. He looked around the yard at the half-dozen dead or injured men. Two horses struggled on the ground and a third had taken refuge on the wide stoop of the house. Other doors began to open and the rest of the Payne men emerged with looks of triumph on their faces.

Joe and Fred had Winchesters in their hands and Betty carried a shotgun which she had already used to good effect. The two young children pulled aside the pale curtains to enjoy the scene while they watched their father finish off the two injured animals.

Joe ordered the wounded men to be taken to the bunkhouse and looked after. He and his brother gathered up the fallen weapons and began stripping the harnesses off the dead horses. They grinned at each other as they worked.

'I don't reckon as how we'll get any more arguments about payin' to use the valley,' Fred said contentedly. 'Them folks sure as hell ran for cover. And they won't be back.'

Betty had gone to the bunkhouse to tend the wounded and the two brothers looked round their kingdom with the sense of a job well done.

One of the hands came across with a broad grin on his face.

'I reckon we was ready for them, Mr Payne,' he said with a certain private smile. 'They didn't stand no chance, did they.'

Joe took the hint and picked out an almost new Winchester and a quantity of ammunition. The man took it gratefully. He had been out on the north range and had seen the second group heading for the valley. Sensing that something was wrong, he had galloped for home and warned the Paynes. They had quickly gathered what was left of their hands and set an ambush in case the ranchers broke through and attacked the house. It had worked beautifully.

'You earned that, fella,' Joe told the man and sent him off to see what had happened at the south entrance to the spread. Black Jack should have put up a fight there, but he now seemed to have vanished and the rancher was a bit worried. Jack Neville was their ace in the hole, and without him, the day might come when the local cattlemen could feel brave enough to try another raid. Joe wished that his father would turn up to start taking charge of things.

'Where the hell is Jack Neville?' he said aloud without even realizing it. Fred just shrugged and walked towards the house, laden down with guns.

Jack Neville had left his hiding-place and was heading south. He had not walked much more than a mile or so when he heard the thunder of horses behind him. He looked back towards the valley and saw a group of riders coming at a smart pace. He ducked among the long grasses and lay silently until they were well past. He had recognized some of them as being the men who had ridden into the valley from the southern end. They now seemed to be in full flight. That was not what he had expected, and he stood watching their dust-cloud with uncertainty on his thin face.

They must have raided the ranch house. It was the only way things could have turned out. But they now seemed to be a defeated and undisciplined gang, flying for their lives. He also reckoned that there were not as many as he would have expected to see. He had certainly heard some shooting and it looked as though they had been on the wrong end of most of it.

Jack Neville thought about going back to the Payne spread. He needed a horse, and he would be out of a job with only the money in his pocket to support him until another one came along. But going back could be the wrong move. The Payne brothers might think he had let them down. The hired gun shrugged ruefully and decided to go on walking to somewhere where he could sell his gold watch and buy himself a mount. Jack Neville did not go in for horse-stealing. He had enough pride to take only the horses of folk he killed.

He had walked the best part of seven miles by the time the sun went down. There was no water around and he simply curled up in the lee of some bushes and tried to sleep. The insects pestered him and eventually he kindled a fire and sat miserably in front of it until he dozed off just as dawn was breaking. He set off again, hungry, thirsty, and covered in a fine dust from the steady wind.

He stopped once to tear up some lush grass and chew it to give his mouth a little moisture. It was then that he saw a lone rider approaching from the south.

# ELEVEN

Wes Roberts was in no hurry to reach the twin buttes that guarded the valley across the Payne land. He rode slowly, camping for the night and setting off just after dawn the next morning. He saw the crowd of horsemen riding wildly off towards the east and was a bit puzzled by the sight.

By the time he had pulled out the old spyglass and got it focused on the dust-trailed group, it was not possible to recognize anybody. He put the telescope away slowly and sat watching them disappear as the land dipped and their dust covered the trail.

He was travelling so slowly that he made camp for a second night and set off again just after dawn. The sun began to climb as he neared the rearing towers of rock that marked the entrance to the disputed land. He thought that he saw some movement in the distance and shaded his eyes to get a better view. A solitary figure was walking slowly towards him.

Wes Roberts speeded up his mount and was confronting the man just a few minutes later. The walker was tall and thin, in dust-covered clothes and with a gun on each hip. He carried no supplies and was chewing a few blades of grass. Wes reached for the leather water-bottle and passed it down to the man without speaking.

The stranger spat out the grass, nodded his thanks, and took a long swig from the bottle before passing it back.

'That was a mighty welcome drink, young fella,' he said as he wiped his mouth.

'What are you doin' out here on foot?' the marshal asked as he hung the bottle back on the pommel. 'Somebody steal your horse?'

The man grinned ruefully.

'You could say that. I sure as sure had to leave it behind. There weren't no time to saddle up and get the hell out all nice and peaceful. Where's you heading, Marshal?'

'The valley. I aim to see if that fence is still there.'

The man grinned and his white teeth showed up in the dark face.

'Well, it ain't,' he said. 'A gang of fellas pulled most of it down and I figure as they then rode on to the Payne homestead and done a bit more damage there.'

Wes Roberts was looking at the man carefully. He had never seen Jack Neville but he had a feeling that they were just making acquaintance. Two guns, a thin, tall fellow, and an air of confidence that goes with experience.

'And you were workin' for the Paynes?' he asked.

'Sure was, but we was bushwhacked back there and shot up real bad. I figure as how I just lost a good job.'

'At least you're still alive.'

The man grinned again.

'And I aim to stay that way.'

He advanced to the head of the marshal's horse and put his hand on its neck to stroke it gently.

'And I need me a horse right now, lad,' he said, 'so if you don't mind just steppin' down, we can do business.'

Wes swung his mount away from the stroking fingers.

'You have to be joking, fella,' he said breathlessly. 'Are you goin' in for horse-stealin' now?'

Jack Neville's head jerked back angrily.

'I ain't no horse-thief, lad,' he snapped. 'I play fair. I need a horse right now and you got one. So we deal. I've got a gold watch here and ten dollars. That's a fair trade for any man and I don't aim to raise the payment. So just get down off there and take the money. Then we can both

109

go our ways in peace.'

Wes Roberts was scared but he tried not to show it. To lose his horse and saddle would make him the laughing-stock of Coville. But the alternative seemed to be about losing his life. He knew that there was a decision to make And he made it.

The marshal swung his horse round and dismounted. He let the reins touch the ground so that the well-trained animal would stay in position. Then he advanced to within a few feet of his opponent.

'I ain't sellin' and you ain't buyin',' he said quietly. 'Why don't you just go on your way?'

The man looked at the young marshal with an expression of complete surprise.

'Do you know who I am, lad?' he asked.

'I do. You're a hired gun who scares the hell outa folk because you're fast on the draw. Well, I'm a hired gun too, so if you fancy drawin' on me, you'll never get a better chance.'

Black Jack Neville had not expected that. He shook his head in disbelief as his fist lowered towards the right-hand holster.

'You sure is one hell of a crazy kid,' he murmured as the gun leapt out and the click of the hammer sounded loud in the thin air.

He was not fast enough. Wes Roberts used the expertise that he had practised in front of glass bottles on a fence for years. The hammer was already back on his gun as he drew it. That fraction of timing was enough and Black Jack staggered backwards, stunned more by surprise than by the blast of the shot in his chest. He stared unbelievingly at his opponent, then at the blood that seeped down his dusty shirt.

'You're one hell of a crazy kid,' he murmured as he slid to the ground.

The ranch house was back to normal when Wes Roberts rode in. One of the hands was saddling a horse, Betty was beating some mats hung from a line, and the two children were playing happily over by one of the barns.

'Well, you've missed all the excitement.' Betty greeted him cheerfully as he dismounted. 'Did you pass the Indians fleein' for their lives from the blue-belly cavalry?'

Wes grinned.

'I saw some ranchers gallopin' off, but they sure tore up all your fencin' before you scared 'em to hell. Is Joe around?'

'In the house. And you're just in time for fresh coffee.'

She led the way indoors where the brothers were sitting at the table with a meal in front of them. They appeared a little uneasy but were eager enough to talk of the way they had beaten the ranch owners and driven them off Payne land.

Wes listened patiently as he sipped the strong, fresh brew.

'So all your problems is solved,' he suggested when they had told their story. 'You'll put back the fence and keep chargin' for cattle to go through the valley?'

The two young men were silent and it was Betty who eventually answered the question.

'We'll have to think about it,' she said. 'I reckon that enough folk have died over this already.'

Wes nodded.

'Maybe it weren't such a good idea. What does your pa say about it?'

He watched the reactions of the three startled faces.

'Pa's dead,' Joe said flatly. 'You was at his funeral.'

Wes shook his head.

'I traced Bill Dean and his bank in Watona. Saw the place he lives and had a run-in with the local marshal. He was one real protective fella. Didn't want to tell me a thing about your pa.'

The two brothers looked at each other. It was Joe who eventually answered.

'Some other old fella was killed in Abilene, so Pa decided to retire,' he said slowly. 'We pay him some money every month and he lives with Uncle Jesse at that place you found. Pa's scared the Smith brothers might still be after him, and he ain't takin' no chances. After all, he's an old man.'

'Two of the Smiths are dead. That only leaves Abie,' Wes said musingly. 'And your pa is gonna have to come alive again if he wants to save half the ranch from goin' to Jeannie Jones. You got yourselves one real problem there, fella.'

'I know,' Joe nodded glumly. 'We sent Pa a signal to come back here and talk it over. He ain't turned up yet.'

'Maybe he's out there stalkin' the last of the Smiths,' Wes suggested.

Nobody denied the possibility.

It was Fred who took up the conversation again.

'You said you had a run-in with Marshal Brady,' he growled. 'I'm a bit surprised you lived to get out of Watona. He's one tough man, is Uncle Jim.'

Wes Roberts grinned.

'Uncle Jim, is it? Well, that explains his concern for your pa. He wasn't all that tough, Fred. Too slow on the draw.'

He was pleased to see the surprise and sudden respect on their faces.

'You killed him?' It was Betty who murmured the words very quietly.

'Had to. I hope he ain't too much a part of the family.'

'One of Ma's brothers,' Joe said in a dull voice.

'So is Uncle Jesse, where Pa stays. They ain't real kin. We never met 'em, in fact. But Pa is among folk he knows, and that helps. Even the fella in the Watona bank is some kin to Ma.'

Wes stood up to go.

'Well, I gotta report to the mayor,' he said formally. 'He'll be glad to hear that you've changed your mind about chargin' folk to use the valley next season. It's bad for the town, and like Betty says, there's been too much killin' already. And now that you ain't got Black Jack Neville, I reckon the local ranchers won't be scared off no more.'

'Jack's still around,' Joe said without conviction.

'He's dead,' Wes told him bluntly. 'I've got his guns across my saddle. If you don't make peace with your neighbours, Joe, they'll be down on this place like the whole Apache Nation.'

All three stared at the young marshal with stunned faces. He suddenly realized just how much respect the killing of a man like Neville could produce.

'You killed Jack Neville?' Fred said slowly.

'A few miles south of here. He had no horse and thought he could buy mine. If you want to bury him, you'll find the body up by that ridge where the mesquite's in full bloom.'

He was treated with equal honour when he

114

returned to Coville. The mayor presided over a small council-meeting while Wes made his report on events out at Twin Buttes. The faces of the councilmen were a study as they began to assess the toughness of their new marshal. The young man was suddenly being treated with a respect he had never known in his life. He was a big man in his home town and even his uncle eyed him differently.

The news he brought was welcome and the meeting soon broke up after a celebration round of drinks. Wes left the saloon with a few slaps on the back. He found himself in the company of Will Fortnum as he walked back to the jailhouse.

'You impressed them back there, fella,' the banker said in his smooth voice. 'A gunslinging marshal is what every town needs to ensure law and order. Tell me, Wes, are you figuring on keeping this job?'

They had reached the stoop of the marshal's office and the young man looked at the banker with an expression of puzzlement.

'Why in hell not?' he asked. 'I reckon I've got a reputation now. And the money's as good as I'm ever likely to earn.'

Will Fortnum pulled a wry face and looked round to make sure that other folk could not hear what was being said.

'Lookit, Wes,' he murmured confidentially,

'I've known you since you were a lad, and I knew your folks as well. Being a lawman is a good job. But one with a reputation for being a fast draw is a different thing altogether. Every gunslinger for a hundred miles around is like to visit Coville. He'll want to see the young fella who killed Jack Neville.'

He put a hand on the marshal's arm.

'And he'll want to prove to the world that he can outshoot him,' he finished.

There was a silence between the two men for a while as they both stood watching a wagon go past with a couple of noisy mules being prodded on their way with too heavy a load.

'But what can I do about it, Mr Fortnum?' Wes asked as he considered the matter. 'It's a job and I got nothing' else. Besides, I owe it all to Uncle Nathan.'

'You owe nothing to your Uncle Nathan. He's using you, lad. Just as he uses this whole town. Now, if I was a young fella with no ties, I'd be saving all the money that came my way, and when I had a thousand dollars or so, I'd be getting a bank loan and heading west to homestead some government land and start my own spread. And I wouldn't be telling folks how good I was with a gun. Think about it, Wes.'

'Mr Fortnum, you're givin' me some strange advice,' the marshal said thoughtfully, 'and I'm sure grateful. But it ain't like you. Not one little bit. This town has protection with me as marshal, and that makes your bank a safer place. I ain't sayin' as how I disagree, but I just don't see what you're gettin' out of it.'

The banker laughed, and in genuine amusement rather than as the performance he used for business purposes.

'You sure as hell know me, Wes,' he said cheerfully. 'But for once in my selfish life, I'm giving advice that doesn't make me money. Use your position, son, and stow away every cent until you can leave this place behind and start afresh. I've seen too much killing in my lifetime, and I'm beholden to your ma and pa. I don't aim to see you preached over by some drunken Holy Joe. Get out, son. While you can.'

The banker went on his way with a feeling of pious satisfaction. He had not thought it necessary to explain that a marshal who was kin to the mayor was not a good thing for other folk in business.

# TWELVE

The Smith ranch house was a large, adobe structure. It was roofed in rust-coloured tiles that sprouted a few stalks of grass here and there. There were three iron stovepipes and fine windows curtained with new drapes. It was a prosperous-looking place and formed one side of a courtyard flanked by barns, a bunkhouse and a workshop.

Abie Smith was a frightened man. He stayed inside and only the foreman was admitted to receive his orders. The three Smith brothers had looked after each other all their lives, but now he was the only one left. He felt scared, and his large hand was never far from a shotgun that lay on the table in the darkened room. The shutters were drawn and the oil-lamps burned all day.

Everybody seemed to have heard that the Payne brothers had hired Black Jack Neville to take revenge for the death of their father. Abie

Smith spent each day behind locked doors and knew that his own ranch hands were not to be relied upon in an emergency. Jack Neville's reputation had them all cowed.

But good news arrived early one Monday morning. The hands had been been paid that weekend and most of them had gone into the nearest town to sample its delights. The telegraph had been busy and word was out that the marshal of some little place south of them had killed the feared gunslinger. The men could hardly wait to take the news back to their boss.

Abie Smith drew a huge sigh of relief. The shutters were flung open, he breathed in the fresh air, and even decided to venture out to see how his huge ranch was prospering. Black Jack was not an easy man to replace. The Payne brothers might think again before tangling with professional guns who attracted the attention of a good lawman.

He oversaw some branding, checked the purity of a creek that was running a little discoloured, and returned to the ranch house with a lighter heart and a bigger appetite than usual.

There was still one other worry, which would not go away quite as easily. His brother Ned had been carrying the cattle-sale money when he was killed. It had vanished, and Abie had to assume that Jack Neville had taken it. That money was needed and the loss meant that there would have to be another cattle-drive before the end of the year. He hated the thought. The animals were not ready and prices would have dropped.

Two or three weeks after this Abie Smith ventured out to the local town with his hands. He had a few drinks and returned home content with the world. He took no notice of the old man in the saloon and was not aware that he and his men had been followed back to the ranch by the bearded, unwashed figure who lived under the name of Bill Dean and was biding his time before killing the last of the Smiths.

Harry Payne made camp on a wooded ridge above the ranch house. He saw the smoke curling from one of the iron stovepipes just after dawn and sniffed the frying of bacon. He could see the hands washing at the pump and their voices floated in the air to where he lay with a spyglass in his gnarled fist.

The old man grinned as the men left for work and only Abie was still around. He could be seen passing behind the window of the ranch house as he drank from a white coffee-mug. The door of the large building was ajar to let in the fresh morning air. Abie Smith could be heard shouting at a small dog that scampered out of the house as if a boot had been applied in a tender place.

Harry Payne scanned the area to see if any of

the hands still lingered near enough to be dangerous. His horse was near by for a quick escape and he had no intention of failing at such a late stage. The last of the Smith brothers was going to die as planned.

There was some movement down by one of the barns and Harry focused the spyglass. A bent old man was emerging from the large barn with an armful of harness. He carried it across the yard to the workshop and pushed the heavy door open. Harry focused the glass on the house again. There was no movement now and he looked carefully around for signs of life. Only the old man closing the workshop door and disappearing from sight disturbed the stillness of the scene.

Harry Payne crawled back over the ridge and sat thinking about the situation. If he went down to the house and killed Abie, the old man would come tearing out of the workshop with the gun that he carried on his hip. It would be easy enough to shoot him but Harry had no quarrel with anybody other than Abie Smith.

He crawled back to the crown of the ridge and used the glass to examine the workshop. There was a large hook and eye to secure the door. If he could get down there and lock the old man in the whole business would soon be over. Even if the man started shouting and hammering it would not matter. Abie would come out of the house and meet his executioner anyway.

The old rascal chuckled as he went back to his horse and walked it quietly round the base of the slope until he ended up behind the empty bunkhouse. He tethered it there, took off his spurs, and silently moved across the courtyard, bending double as he passed the ranch house windows.

He could hear the elderly hand inside the workshop as he lifted the hook and placed it gently in the staple. That done, he straightened up and stepped confidently across the yard to the ranch house.

The door was already ajar and he found himself in a warm, well-furnished room that smelt strongly of food. There were two closed doors in the opposite wall and an open door to the left. He could see the kitchen stove through the open door, but the main room was empty.

As Harry hesitated one of the other doors opened and Abie Smith lumbered into the room with a pair of boots in his large hands. There was a moment of suspense between the two men as they stared at each other.

'Who the hell are you?' Abie Smith growled angrily. 'I don't reckon to saddle tramps hornin' into my home, fella.'

'I'm your killer, Abie,' Harry Payne grinned through his scruffy beard. 'Harry Payne's come back for you.'

He drew the .44 as the big man raised his arms to throw the boots across the room. Harry pulled the trigger and sent his enemy spinning round. He fired again and the man dropped to the floor.

Harry stared down at the body for a moment and then turned to leave. He was satisfied now. All the Smiths were dead and their sister inherited the land. When she died it would all go to his sons and the Payne family would be the biggest ranchers in the whole of the south. He was still grinning as he closed the door behind him and limped towards the spot where his horse was hidden. He could hear the rattling of the workshop door and the shouts of the old man who was trying to get out.

What Harry did not hear was the opening of the house door again and the drawing back of the hammers of a shotgun. The weapon blasted off with deadly force and the explosion was repeated as the other barrel was fired. Harry Payne staggered forward to fall flat on the ground with gaping wounds in his back. He never moved again. It was a woman who had fired. She was in her fifties, well-built and neatly dressed in a striped-cotton frock covered by an apron.

Jeannie Jones, formerly Smith, tucked the shotgun under her arm and walked slowly towards the body. She looked down with a slightly puzzled look on her face before turning towards the noise that was coming from the rattling door of the workshop. She crossed the yard slowly and unhooked it. The old man practically fell out, a gun in his hand and his eyes watering with the effort.

'It's all right, Eli,' she said soothingly. 'I've got the fella. You can put your gun away.'

'What happened, Ma?' the man asked in a wheezy voice.

'I don't rightly know. I was just prettyin' myself up when I hears the shootin' in the parlour. By the time I loaded the gun, Abie was lyin' dead on the floor and this fella was headin' for the hills.'

The old man leaned over the corpse and stirred it gently with his foot.

'You sure blasted him to hell and back,' he chuckled.

She nodded and looked round the yard.

'He must have a horse somewhere close by,' she murmured. 'We gotta find it. And while you're on kickin' terms with the fella, go through his pockets and see what he's got.'

The old man did as he was told and presented the woman with a handful of money, a watch, and some papers. She handed him the shotgun and counted the cash.

'Twenty-seven dollars,' she mused. 'He ain't a saddle tramp, that's for sure. And this watch is

124

gold. We got ourselves a well-paid fella here, Eli.'

She handed the papers back to the man.

'I ain't got my glasses. Can you tell me what these is all about?'

'I ain't got my glasses either,' Eli said sheepishly. It was better than admitting that he could not read.

Jeannie Jones unfolded one of the pieces of paper and held it close to her eyes. Her mouth formed the words and a puzzled expression passed over her face.

'Well, if that don't beat all,' she muttered. 'This fella is called Bill Dean and this here is from a bank in Watona. Where the hell is Watona?'

'South of here. Near Milligan's Creek.'

'Oh. Well, this here bank pays him cash regular-like, and the folk who foot the bill are Harry Payne's sons. They hired this old goat to kill my brothers. They even paid him an extra ten dollars after Ned's death.'

'I thought folk said that Jack Neville was hired to do that job, Ma.'

'That sure as hell is what we all believed,' she admitted, 'but this lists monthly payments and they go back quite a ways. Back before Alex was killed. I guess Abie let down his guard too soon.'

She looked at the bank statement again and suddenly let out an unladylike curse.

'It was this fella what got our cattle money,'

she snarled. 'He paid that exact amount into that bank in Watona. Now we ain't got a coon's chance in hell of ever gettin' it back.'

She turned on her heel and stormed towards the house while Eli stood with the shotgun under his arm and the dead body at his feet.

'What are we gonna do about him?' he whined plaintively. 'I can't move him by myself.'

'The hands can get him underground when they come in for a meal,' Jeannie Jones shouted back over her shoulder. 'But look around the place for his horse. We can use every cent the old devil was worth.'

'Are you gonna be runnin' things now, Ma?' Eli asked a little fearfully.

She stopped in her tracks. With all the excitement and then the bad news about the stolen money, Jeannie had forgotten her new position.

'Yes,' she said slowly. 'I reckon I will be. And you know, Eli, this old goat might have been a hired gun, but he sure as hell made me the richest woman you're ever like to meet in these parts.'

# THIRTEEN

Some of the news came from the driver and guard of the stage. They told of the death of the last Smith brother and the rumour that he had been killed by a gunslinger hired by the Payne family. More news came by telegraph, confirming the story of the shooting. Coville was delighted with the new gossip. It was better than the tale of the preacher being so drunk that he fell into the hole when burying old Ma Swainson.

'It don't make sense,' Nathan Laird moaned as he sat with the marshal and Banker Fortnum. 'That woman now has all the Smith land and half the Payne ranch. Unless Harry really is alive.'

'And even then she has all the Smith land and is like to outlive Harry.' Will Fortnum pondered. 'What do you think, Wes?'

There was a time when the banker would

never have consulted the young lawman. But that was before he had killed Black Jack Neville. Wes Roberts weighed his words carefully.

'Harry and this wife of his could be in it together,' he suggested, 'but I don't think his sons are. When I told them of the will, they were real put out. Scared to hell they'd be saddled with her. But if Harry is still alive, now's the time he'll show up. If he and her is partners, he's got to turn his hand to runnin' all the spreads. He can't just sit back and let her take over, can he? It's hardly a woman's job.'

Banker Fortnum nodded his head slowly.

'You could be right,' he said. 'So what do we do now?'

'Nothing.' The mayor's voice was firm. 'We just wait and see. We need to get things back to normal, and I reckon this is the time. Everything will quieten down, so let's not be too hasty. If the Paynes just treat their neighbours decently, and give this woman her share of the profits, we can all live at peace.'

A couple of hours later more news came in over the telegraph line. Abie Smith's killer had a name. He was called Bill Dean and had been shot by Abie's widowed sister. The stolen cattle money also got a mention. There was another hasty meeting in the mayor's office as the First Citizen poured consoling glasses of whiskey for the banker and the marshal.

'So she shot her own husband,' he murmured unbelievingly. 'And Harry was the fella going round killing the Smith brothers. If that don't beat all.'

'She didn't know it was her husband,' Wes said softly. 'That means they weren't in it together. If she wasn't his widow before, she sure is now.'

'Unless she let him kill them and then deliberately finished him off,' the banker mused. 'It's one way of grabbing everything.'

The mayor put away the whiskey bottle.

'Well, it seems to be all finished,' he said. 'The two Payne boys will just have to live with it. Half their spread belongs to the widow and I reckon they got what they deserved.'

They split up shortly afterwards and Wes Roberts went thoughtfully back to the jailhouse. It was not quite all there was to the matter, but some instinct made him keep his ideas to himself.

Things gradually got back to normal in Coville much as the mayor had predicted. The ranch hands came into town when they were paid and the stores started to do more trade as the money from the cattle sales began to circulate. Even the Payne brothers put in an appearance now and then.

They got a few dirty looks but everyone knew that they now only owned half the spread on which they worked. It was a good revenge for the trouble they had caused by their greed.

The trouble flared one Saturday night when the ranch hands were drinking their pay in the saloons and quarrels were starting to spring up, as they usually did.

One started in the mayor's saloon when a couple of hands from a neighbouring ranch began fighting amid a shower of spilled drinks and broken glasses. A few others joined in and one of the bartenders tried to stop it with a pick-axe-handle. He was knocked down for his pains. The mayor stayed safely upstairs while somebody ran to the marshal's office for help.

Wes Roberts was already out patrolling Coville and keeping an eye on the other saloon, where he had earlier stopped two fights amid the applause of the other drinkers. The messenger eventually found him and delivered the news that he was wanted urgently in the Southern Star. Wes hurried down the main street and could hear the noise before he even got near the place.

He flung back the swing-doors and entered to find a scene of chaos. One man lay on the sawdusted floor, bleeding from a head wound. Another was crouched in a chair, holding a damaged arm. Four more were still fighting, two of them with knives and the other pair with their bare fists.

'All right! That's enough!' the marshal roared.

He now knew from experience that it would be enough. The sight of him was sufficient to tame the meanest drunk. But nothing happened. He yelled again. One pair of fighters split up and their friends were able to part them. The other two were still armed with knives and ignored him completely.

Before Wes could do anything one of the men lunged with the large knife and caught his opponent across the knuckles. The man let out a yell and dropped his own weapon. It clattered on to the floor and he stood defenceless for a moment.

His antagonist let out a drunken whoop of delight and lunged again. The knife buried itself to the hilt in the man's waist, just above the belt. A sudden silence fell on the saloon as everybody sobered up and stood stricken by the fatal outcome. They watched the injured man clutching his stomach as he staggered backwards for a few feet before collapsing.

The drunk looked round with an expression of triumph on his dark, unshaven face. Nobody challenged him until Wes Roberts stepped forward.

'Drop that knife,' the marshal ordered firmly. 'I'm takin' you in for murder.'

'Murder!' The killer's eyes blazed. 'You gotta be loco, young fella. We fought clean and he got what he deserved for callin' me a no-good drunk. That ain't murder.'

'He was unarmed,' the marshal said bluntly. 'He ain't even carryin' a gun.'

The man stared for a moment and then looked around the saloon for sympathetic backing. There was none, and he realized that he stood alone. He decided to brazen it out and flipped the large bloodstained knife from one hand to the other.

'And you think I'm gonna let a young punk like you take me?' he sneered. 'I've ate fellas like you for breakfast, lad. Now, get back to the schoolroom and learn your letters.'

He looked round for applause but the saloon was still silent.

'Drop it or I'll drop you.'

The marshal's voice was hard and his hand moved just above the gun at his side. The room lay hushed. Nathan Laird had come to the top of the stairs now that he knew Wes Roberts was in charge of the situation.

The knifeman's dark eyes moved hungrily from side to side. He was looking for help from his friends. He had none and was all alone to give up or brazen it out. The knife clattered to the floor and his right hand dropped to the gun at his waist. He was too late.

Marshal Roberts drew with lightning speed and fired one shot. His opponent opened his mouth as though to say something. Then he slid against the bar and collapsed slowly to the floor.

Nathan Laird came down the stairs and patted his nephew on the shoulder. He looked round at his customers as a broad smile lit his face.

'Drinks all round,' he boomed. 'We got law and order in this town and we're letting the world know it.'

Wes put away his gun and walked out of the saloon.

The mayor stood watching him leave, and then, after a slight hesitation, decided to follow his nephew across the street to the jailhouse. He made it just as Wes was closing the door.

'You're upset about this, lad,' Nathan challenged in a kindly voice.

'Yes, in a way,' the marshal answered. 'I don't like goin' round killin' folk, Uncle Nathan, and that's a fact. Bein' a lawman ain't all it's cracked up to be.'

'Few jobs are. But what you did tonight is like to stop other fellas from making free with knives and guns. Those two hellions should have had more sense. They both work for Wally Williams, by the way. He's not going to be pleased at you shooting one of his foremen like that. If he's in town tonight, we'll be hearing from him soon.'

Wes picked up the coffee-pot from the stove and offered a cup to his uncle.

'Wally Williams was shot up at the Payne

133

spread, wasn't he?' he asked.

'Yes. Right arm and shoulder. Doc Hawson took out quite a collection of buckshot.'

'Then he won't be comin' here with a gun, I reckon.'

The mayor pulled a face.

'Well, he's got a bad temper, and he's left-handed.'

# FOURTEEN

Nothing much happened for the next few days. The stage came and went as usual and Wes noticed that a small, dark man alighted and headed in the direction of Coville's better hotel. He was a dapper little fellow in well-cut clothes and with a stovepipe hat that sat atop a pale, thin face.

The marshal instantly reckoned him for somebody in the legal profession. This seemed to be confirmed the next day when he was seen coming out of Judge Crawford's office accompanied by Lawyer Mason. Will Fortnum also appeared to be interested in the man; he was watching events from the doorway of his bank. He and the marshal exchanged glances across the street and he eventually appeared at the jail-house door.

'I was wondering who our visitor was,' the banker said a little uncertainly. 'Do you know anything, Wes?'

The marshal shook his head.

'No, but somethin' is goin' on that must be important. That fella came all the way from Abilene.'

'Did he now?' The moneylender screwed up his eyes in thought. 'Sounds as if you've already been asking around, young fella.'

'I looked in at the Wells Fargo office.' Wes grinned. 'It doesn't do for a lawman to be ignorant about things in his town.'

'No, indeed.'

The banker helped himself to coffee and sat down on the opposite side of the old desk.

'Those events the other night in the saloon,' he mused. 'You are going to have that sort of thing all your working life. Have you thought more about settling a place of your own somewheres else, as we were discussing?'

'You were discussing, as I recall,' the marshal said with a slight smile. 'It was almost as though you was tryin' to get rid of me, Mr Fortnum.'

The banker laughed.

'A fool you're not, young Wes,' he said cheerfully. 'Look, lad, your uncle is a powerful man in this town and he uses everybody. But we're expanding, and other folks have rights as well as Nathan Laird. With a marshal who is kin to him, and beholden to him, that doesn't leave the rest of us with much authority around the place. You see my point?'

Wes nodded. 'I sure do,' he said, 'but what exactly are you suggesting? I'd need a lotta cash money to start a new life with a homestead, cattle, and all the other things I'd have to have.'

The banker leaned forward across the desk.

'Well, as I said, if you could raise about a thousand dollars, the bank would then regard you as somebody worth investing in. We could make you a decent loan. I could also give you a guide about buying the right spread. You might end up a big rancher. With the proper help.'

'A thousand dollars is a lotta money, Mr Fortnum. I can't earn that in a coupla years, let alone save it.'

'I know, lad, but that's the way things work. We've got to know that you're a sound investment. Just bear it in mind. There are things that happen in your line of work that might help. Think it over.'

'I will.'

It was the same afternoon that Wally Williams finally came to town. He was one furious man who had lost two good hands, was in pain with his arm wound, and who felt humiliated by what had happened out at the Payne ranch. He was in no mood to let things blow over in a town which, he felt, should have supported the local ranchers more than it had done.

He headed straight for the mayor and registered some bitter complaints. Nathan Laird listened fearfully, eyeing the gun at Wally's side and knowing that he had arrived in town with two of his hands to back him up. The mayor had given the nod to one of his bartenders and the man hurried across to the marshal's office to break the bad news.

Wes heaved a heavy sigh and walked across the street to the saloon. Nathan was standing a few steps up on the stairs, towering over the rancher but clearly at a disadvantage. His eyes brightened at the sight of his nephew and his glance made Wally Williams turn around.

'So here comes the hero who goes round killin' my hands,' Wally bellowed. 'You sure is one fine lawman. You do nothin' to stop the Payne brothers from closin' the range, but you go killin' honest folk when they're just havin' a bit of a set-to after a few drinks. I gotta mind to put a bullet in you here and now, young fella.'

'That would be a mistake, Mr Williams,' Wes said quietly. 'It wouldn't solve anythin' and I'd be shootin' back. You know as well as any man that the town marshal's got no powers out on the free range. And I don't doubt your hands have already told you about the fight here the other night. A bit of a set-to ain't the word for it. An unarmed man was stabbed to death.'

'Them's the facts, Wally,' Nathan chipped in. 'I saw it all for myself. You have to be reasonable about these things.'

'Reasonable! I'm down two good men, and made to look like some rube who can be chased round the corral by a stray coyote.'

'So what do you intend to do about it, Mr Williams?'

Wes's voice was still quiet and steady, but there was a steely note to it and the other two men stared at him for a moment. It was the rancher who spoke.

'Well, I sure as hell ain't takin' that sort of uppity talk from a kid like you,' he snarled.

His left hand went down to the gun at his belt. It never touched the butt as he reeled back against the stair rail and bumped into Nathan Laird. Wes Roberts had drawn first and did not miss.

The marshal ignored the falling man and turned swiftly towards the door of the saloon. He had seen the two men sitting their horses there when he entered. He knew who they were and that they were supposed to back up their boss should the need arise.

They came tearing through the door as he levelled his gun, but stopped in their tracks when they saw the marshal ready to open fire. Their hands went clear of the holsters as they looked at their boss lying on the floor.

'Go along to Doc Hawson and tell him that Mr Williams is hurt bad,' Wes ordered them.

'There's no need,' the mayor said as he bent over the fallen man. 'He's dead.'

'In that case you can sling him across his horse and ride outa town,' the marshal said.

He stood aside as the men meekly did as they were told. They were soon on their way back to the ranch.

Nathan slapped his nephew happily on the shoulder.

'You handled that beautifully, Wes,' he crowed. 'This town is certainly getting a reputation for not standing any gunslinging from folks. I reckon you're the best marshal we ever had.'

Wes looked hard at his uncle before heading for the door.

'Yeah, I'm real pleased with myself,' he muttered.

# FIFTEEN

'The Payne brothers won't come into town.'

It was Judge Crawford who spoke. He lay back in his chair like a dusty black spider in the middle of its web. The two lawyers sat opposite him and Wes Roberts stood in the background. The office was musty with the afternoon heat and cigar smoke that moved in spirals towards the stained ceiling.

'And how far is it to their spread?' asked the visitor to town. His tone was anxious and not the voice of a seasoned traveller. The Judge looked to Wes for guidance.

'If you're usin' a rig,' the marshal said, 'it's a two-day journey, but there's one good waterhole for the night. The trail's pretty well marked.'

'It's all very inconsiderate,' the man grumbled as he took out a large bandanna to mop his brow. 'Why can't these people see sense? Mr Payne's widow has been very patient, but she

141

really is entitled to her share of the cattle prices that were obtained at the last sale. Her husband was dead long before those deals were made.'

'I think she should be more considerate with my clients,' Lawyer Mason snapped. 'What with their father being murdered in Abilene and all this range war, they've not had time to sort things out. After all, they're ranchers, not accountants behind a desk.'

'My client *was* being considerate,' the lawyer snapped back, 'until she uncovered evidence that these two young men had employed this Bill Dean fellow to kill her brothers. He also stole the money that Ned Smith was carrying. We are taking legal action in Watona township to recover that. Unfortunately, I have little hope of success there. It cannot be easily proved that the money came from the Smith funds. But my client can at least insist on her rights to a half-share of the H bar P profits. And that's why I'm here.'

'I do object to your accusing my clients of murdering people,' Lawyer Mason snapped. 'There is no tangible evidence for that at all. I appeal to you, Judge, does the matter have to be dealt with in this antagonistic way?'

Judge Crawford shifted in his seat and stared at the end of his cigar.

'Well, Jack, you represent the Payne boys, so why not put forward something concrete with

142

regard to the money? I've seen all the papers in the case, and I reckon as how the lady is entitled to her share. All you have to do is to get the Paynes to authorize the bank to pay out what's due. I'm sure Mr Bellwood here will agree to that. It would save a journey out to the H bar P.'

'I have not been given authority to make a deal. My clients feel that their elderly father was tricked into a marriage with the widow Jones and that the will he made is not valid.'

The old judge bridled.

'Well, I says it is,' he snapped. 'Old Harry Payne was of as sound a mind as any man I ever clapped eyes on. The will is fair and square and so are the marriage papers. If you ain't prepared to deal, then you can both go out to the Payne spread and talk it over there. The marshal will go with you, just to make sure things ain't likely to take a nasty turn. That all right with you, Wes?'

The young lawman grinned.

'Fine by me, Judge,' he said cheerfully.

Mr Bellwood nodded reluctant agreement.

'If that's the way it must be,' he said sourly, 'then I will make the journey. However, we must wait a day or so. I am expecting to be joined by one of my client's foremen. He is instructed by her to look over the Payne spread and report back on the way it is run and the number of cattle on the place. We will set out when he arrives.'

143

*

Wes Roberts travelled fast across the uneven ground. He wanted to get to the Payne ranch and back to town before he needed to escort the lawyers on their bickering way. He made a report of cattle-rustling an excuse to leave Coville, and the mayor and council had to be content with that.

He was not made very welcome when he arrived. Joe and Fred listened to his tale with stony faces and it was only Betty who really understood the seriousness of all that he reported.

'There's a lot of money involved here,' she said when the tale was told.

'It's not even as simple as that,' Wes told her as he picked up the hot coffee-cup. 'She doesn't know that Bill Dean was not a hired gun. She'd be real mad if she knew it was her own husband killin' off the Smith brothers. The mayor and me worked things out. We done plenty of checking. If she does the same, she might come up with the same answer. I doubt it, but it could happen. However, I got me an idea that might be of help. You could mention it to Jack Mason when he gets here.'

Betty smiled knowingly.

'I wondered why you made this journey,' she said. 'What are you after, Wes?'

144

The marshal grinned.

'I want to get the hell outa Coville,' he told her. 'I need a loan so that I can show the bank I'm worth backin' money to buy my own spread and start in the cattle business.'

'How much of a loan?' It was Joe who spoke.

'A thousand dollars.'

Fred let out a hoot of disgust and Joe shook his head. It was Betty who answered.

'That's a lotta money, Wes,' she said quietly. 'How do we know you'd be payin' it back, and how do we know your information is worth it?'

'Fair question. I'd be dealin' with the Coville bank, so you'd be able to keep tabs on me. As to the information, I think I could get you right out of trouble and you wouldn't have to pay one bent cent to the Smith woman. She wouldn't even be able to claim half your spread.'

Lawyer Mason was looking positively happy when he sat down at the Payne dinner-table with Betty, Fred, and Joe at his side. Lawyer Bellwood was seated opposite them. Wes stood in his usual inferior position near the stove, while the fore-man brought along by Bellwood was somewhere out among the Payne cattle.

Betty and Joe had taken Jack Mason aside when he arrived. They passed on the informa-tion given them by the marshal, and that accounted for the satisfied expression on his face. He listened patiently while the widow's lawyer put his case. Nobody interrupted even though Fred showed impatience at times. His wife laid a restraining hand on his arm and he merely simmered as the man droned on. There was silence when he had finished speaking.

'There is one slight point I would raise,' Lawyer Mason said in moderate tones, 'and it refers to the death of Mr Payne. There is no evidence for that.'

Lawyer Bellwood opened his mouth in astonishment.

'You've got Harry Payne buried in the family plot,' he protested. 'He was killed in Abilene and brought back here. Everybody knows that.'

Lawyer Mason was enjoying himself.

'A body was brought back here and buried, as you say,' he conceded, 'but I suggest that it was not the body of Mr Payne.'

'Then who the hell is it?' The man looked wildly round the room.

'We don't know, but we are quite prepared to have it dug up for identification. You see, Mr Bellwood, Harry Payne limped. He was shot in the right leg during the late war. The limb was broken, and the body in that grave has not a repaired fracture of the right leg. I feel that if we bring out a medical man to check on it, we will find that an unknown person was buried. We also have a note from the owner of the Abilene hotel that tells of her deliberately identifying an unknown body as being that of Mr Payne.'

'So where is Harry Payne?' the lawyer asked hoarsely. 'You're suggesting that he's still alive?'

'There is no proof of his death,' Jack Mason said smugly. 'And that being the case, Mrs Payne is not a widow and the will cannot be enforced.'

'Then why the hell wasn't all this made clear much earlier?' the angry lawyer wanted to know.

'I've only just heard of it myself, but I think that you, and your foreman should leave this family in peace. After all, Mr Payne could turn up at any time. I am told that the reason he chose to vanish was because of his fear. The Smith brothers might have tried to murder him again. Perhaps he can return safely to his loved ones now that they are dead. And perhaps to his wife. I suggest you go and break the good news to her. She is not a sorrowing widow after all.'

Wes Roberts sat in the office of the Coville bank two days later. He looked forlornly at the $200 in his hand and placed it on the desk in front of Will Fortnum.

'It isn't enough, lad,' the banker said ruefully, 'though I'm a bit surprised you managed to raise so much. Been robbing one of our other branches?'

He tried to make light of the situation but the look on the young man's face made him change his mind. Wes Roberts told the story reluctantly. When Lawyer Bellwood and his companion left the Payne ranch, the marshal had expected to get an order on the Coville bank for the thousand dollars agreed.

But Joe and Fred had refused. Betty seemed to be ashamed of what was happening but said nothing. The most that they would offer was $200 in cash, and no more. Joe reminded the young lawman that they were the ones who had the letter from Abilene and that the idea would have come from them sooner or later, anyway.

There was almost violence, but Wes was outgunned and left with the only consolation that was on offer.

'They certainly treated you badly,' the banker said when the story was finished. 'You'll just have to save, lad, and hope for some other windfall.'

He mused for a moment as he tapped the large desk with his fat fingers.

'You, me, and the mayor are the only people in Coville who know that Harry Payne is dead,' he muttered almost to himself, 'and we're the only folk who know that the woman really is a widow. If it were to be let slip . . .'

Wes looked up and saw the crafty expression on the banker's face.

'You really do want me out of Coville, Mr Fortnum,' he said with a weak grin. 'Got another lawman in mind?'

The banker smiled.

'I've got a nephew,' he said.

'That figures.'

# SIXTEEN

Banker Fortnum was a great one for doing his civic duty. Particularly when he thought it would be to his own profit. That evening found him calling at the two saloons, taking a quiet drink and looking around for Lawyer Bellwood. The man was nowhere to be seen and Will Fortnum decided to try the hotel.

He found his quarry sitting at a table in the foyer with a pot of coffee and plate of ham in front of him. The banker introduced himself and sat down.

'The word around town is that you've had a problem with establishing the death of Harry Payne,' he said tentatively.

The lawyer looked at him suspiciously and swallowed a mouthful of coffee.

'What interest could you have in my affairs?' he asked in a hostile manner.

'Oh, as a banker with a knowledge of what

150

goes on around here, I might be able to help.'

The lawyer's hooded eyes opened a little wider.

'How?'

Banker Fortnum rested his hands on the table-top and looked around to make sure that the other few guests were not within earshot.

'The Payne family have their account at my bank,' he said. 'After Harry's death, a monthly payment was ordered to be made to Bill Dean at a bank in Watona.'

'I know all that,' Lawyer Bellwood snapped. 'They hired him to kill the Smith brothers.'

'Harry Payne has a relative near Watona. Somebody they call Uncle Jesse. I happen to know that Harry used to go there now and then. Using the name of Bill Dean.'

The lawyer spilled his coffee on the table and across his shirt front. He put down the cup hurriedly.

'Are you sure of this?' he asked eagerly. 'Bill Dean and Harry Payne are one and the same person?'

The banker nodded.

'Your client shot her own husband back at the Smith place. So she really is his widow. And furthermore, Mr Bellwood, that money in Dean's account at Watona is all part of her inheritance.'

The lawyer's hand was trembling as he shook

the banker's sweaty palm, and Will Fortnum left the hotel contentedly. It was now up to the marshal to play things properly. He had done his bit.

It was two more days before the Payne ranch could be visited again by the lawyers. Nobody was interested in digging up the body in the family plot at this stage. But the widow's attorney was all in favour of checking on the corpse that had been buried on the Smith spread. Joe and Fred were caught, and Lawyer Bellwood left their house with a smirk on his hollow face. A despondent Jack Mason sat beside him on the rig.

It was another two days before Fred Payne reached town. His rage had resisted all attempts on the part of his wife or brother to stop him going into Coville and dealing with the man who must have betrayed their secret. He was set on killing Marshal Roberts.

He stormed into the jailhouse just as Wes was releasing the town drunk and steering him into the street. The man staggered towards the nearest saloon as Fred elbowed past him and confronted the lawman.

'We gave you two hundred dollars, fella!' he yelled, 'and you betrayed us. You told that paper-chewin' lawyer that Pa was Bill Dean. I'm gonna kill you for that.'

Wes shook his head and raised his hands in a gesture of peace.

'I've never even spoken to that lawyer fella,' he said. 'We mixes with a different sort of folk. The mayor knew your secret, Will Fortnum knew, and I wouldn't mind bettin' that the judge was told all about it. These fellas stick together and do what profits them. Nobody asked me any questions, so you go back to the ranch, Fred. I don't want no more killings. That thousand dollars I needed was to get me outa all this. If anyone was betrayed, I was. By you and Joe.'

'You'd better go for that gun, fella. The way you're gettin' outa all this is in a wooden box.'

Fred's hand went down to the holster but never reached it. Wes Roberts's fist hit him full in the face and he staggered back against the door of the jailhouse with blood streaming from his mouth and nose. The marshal took away the gun, threw it on the desk, and before Fred could resist, pushed him into a cell and locked the door.

'Just cool off,' Wes Roberts said tersely as he nursed his grazed knuckles. 'I'll fetch you a meal in an hour or so.'

The marshal went to report to the mayor. The First Citizen listened in mounting anger as he was informed for the first time about the happenings between the Paynes and the lawyers.

'So now we've got the Payne brothers on the

prod again and they're gunning for you, the judge, Will Fortnum, and the Almighty alone knows who else. I want a quiet town here, Wes, and that's what you're paid for.'

'As you say, Uncle Nathan,' the lawman murmured submissively. 'But I thought it best not to involve you. I figure as how Joe Payne is like to show up next. He's a mite smarter than Fred so I might be able to reason with him. Just leave it with me.'

'I'll do that, boy. I don't aim to be mixed up in this. You were right not to tell me what was going on. I've got to be neutral as mayor.'

The marshal left a rather relieved civic head and went along to Doc Hawson to have his hand examined. No bones were broken and he returned to the jailhouse where Fred was sleeping uneasily on the bunk. The doctor had promised to look in on him when he had a chance, but the young rancher did not seem to need any medical help.

A couple of hours later Joe showed up. His horse was weary and its head sagged as he tethered the animal to the rail.

He entered the lamplit jailhouse and brushed some of the dust from off his slicker. The sight of Wes Roberts sitting quietly at his desk seemed to surprise him. He looked across at the bars of the cell and saw his brother eating a meal off a large tin plate.

'I thought you was aimin' to do a little shootin' when you got to town,' he said to him.

Fred looked sheepish and put down the plate to come across to the bars.

'He took me by surprise,' he blustered. 'Get me outa here, Joe.'

Joe Payne almost managed a slight grin as he sat down opposite the unmoving lawman.

'So you got the drop on him, Wes,' he said in a not unfriendly tone. 'You know why he came here, don't you?'

'Sure. He thought I told Lawyer Bellwood about your pa bein' Bill Dean. I never said a word. But other folk knew, and they got their own plans for this town. You and me is just rubber-neckin' on the fringes.'

'Well, whoever talked, we've lost everything, now. Half the spread and half the profits from the last cattle sale. I was sure as hell right not to loan you a thousand dollars. Even that two hundred was too much. We need every cent now.'

'Not loanin' me that thousand dollars was a big mistake, Joe. I ain't friendly no more. I can still get you outa trouble, but the terms is different now. I don't want the loan of a thousand dollars. I just want it as a gift.'

Joe stared at the lawman for a moment. His mouth opened a little and the expression on his face was one of sheer disbelief.

'Fella, you gotta be the biggest fool as ever was,' he murmured hoarsely. 'Why in hell should we give you one bent cent?'

'Because I'm not the wet-behind-the-ears kid some people take me for,' Wes said firmly, 'and I want out of this town and away from folks like you. You've got more sense than Fred here, so take a little advice. Go down the street and dig out that lawyer you use. Jack Mason will be sittin' down to his dinner right now, but get him back here with a copy of the will your pa made out when he married Jeannie Jones.'

'Why the hell. . . ?'

'Just do it, Joe. I'll have some fresh coffee ready by the time you get back.'

The marshal got up from his desk and moved over to the stove. As Joe was opening the door of the office, Wes called him back.

'You might bring Will Fortnum back with you while you're at it,' he said.

'He ain't likely to want to come to the jail-house at this time of night,' Joe said uncertainly.

'I think he will.' The marshal grinned.

The coffee had hardly had a chance to boil before Joe returned. He was accompanied by a smoothly smiling bank manager and a slightly angry lawyer. Both men had been dining when he called on them. The moneylender had will-ingly put on his coat against the chill night air, but the lawyer was more reluctant. It was mention of the will and sheer curiosity that had enticed him from his warm home. He called into his office to collect the will and now laid it in front of him as he sat at the marshal's desk.

'I really must make a protest at being dragged out like this,' he said formally. 'A man in my position . . .'

'The law is draggin' you out, Mr Mason,' Wes said in a hard voice, 'and as marshal of this town, I do not go callin' on folk. They call on me. So let's get down to cases and we can all get to our rest the sooner.'

None of them had ever seen this side of the young man before and only the banker appeared to be enjoying the sight. He nodded his agreement and took the coffee handed to him. Joe did likewise, glumly, while the lawyer haughtily brushed the cup away.

Wes sat down and faced them.

'I'd like to have a look at that will,' he said. 'Just to refresh my memory.'

The lawyer handed it across in cold silence. Wes read it carefully, his mouth forming the words as he did so. Silently he handed it back.

'Your pa was no fool,' the lawman said to Joe. 'He always knew what he was about, and this will proves it. Harry Payne was as cunnin' as a huntin' coyote.'

He looked round at the interested faces.

'So now we come to the way Joe here treated

me when I asked for a loan. I played fair with him because I didn't think some other fella would go talkin' about Harry Payne and Bill Dean bein' one and the same. But Joe let me down, and now we deal business. Cash-on-the-line business.'

'What the hell are you talking about, Marshal?' the lawyer asked impatiently. 'Can you help the Payne family or not?'

'As a lawman,' Wes said carefully, 'I got no interest in this matter. It's a civil case. But I got knowledge and I spent time workin' things out. I used my brains while other folks went around like polecats up a tree. I'll sell my work and my knowledge for one thousand dollars. Take it or leave it.'

'This is outrageous!' Lawyer Mason jumped up from his chair, but Joe pulled him down again and leaned across the desk.

'Wes,' he said slowly, 'if you can get us outa this mess, I'll meet your price. We did go back on our word at the ranch. Betty is as sore as hell about it, and Fred and me ain't lived it down yet. What can we do?'

'You got your banker here, and your lawyer,' Wes said calmly. 'Put everythin' in writing, and when I know I ain't gonna be cheated again, I'll deal my cards.'

Will Fortnum smilingly led the way by taking a pen from the inkwell and going into a discussion

158

with the lawyer and Joe Payne. Wes Roberts sat silently and watched as the nib scratched across the paper and the completed document was passed to him for scrutiny. He nodded his agreement, shook hands with Joe, and picked up the will again. He nursed it between his hands like some precious trinket.

'When the mayor sent me to Watona to check on this Bill Dean fella,' he said, 'I made a few enquiries around the place and was able to go out to the homestead where Uncle Jesse lives. Ever been there, Joe?'

'No, I never met Uncle Jesse. He's some kin to Ma. Brother, I'm told.'

'Well, there ain't no Uncle Jesse. He died a few years back and your pa took up with his widow. Married her fair and square. Her name is Mary and she's content with her life and ain't a woman to make trouble for you.'

'Wait a minute,' the lawyer interrupted. 'Are you telling us that the marriage to the Jones woman was bigamous?'

'Sure was. Old Harry was marryin' her to get his hands on her ranch and on the land her brothers owned. They didn't know he'd actually married her but they were as scared as hell that he would. He was real careful when he made that will though. Real careful.'

He spread out the document and pointed to a line of writing.

'He left half his ranch to his legally wedded wife. But she ain't named.'

'Well, I'll be damned,' Lawyer Mason said softly. 'The cunning old devil. '

'You gotta hand it to Pa,' Fred shouted proudly from the cell.

'You certainly have,' Banker Fortnum smiled. 'I take it that means that the money in the Watona bank goes to the widow of Bill Dean? Mary.'

'We'll have to sort all that out,' Lawyer Mason said cheerfully, 'but I doubt there'll be any argument when everything is explained in proper terms.'

Everybody stood up and there were handshakes all round. Wes Roberts opened the cell door for a grinning Fred to emerge, and stood aside as the two brothers left with their lawyer.

'You worked things out very well, Wes,' Will Fortnum said as he patted the young lawman on the arm.

'I think I may have had a little help somewheres along the line.'

'Well, that's as may be, but we must have a get-together in my office and discuss your future. I think it's going to be a very bright one. You're one real sharp operator, my lad. Real sharp.'

Wes grinned.

'My ma had an old sayin' about it takin' one to know one,' he said.